A HARPER NOVEL OF SUSPENSE

FAGO

A JOAN KAHN BOOK

Books by Berton Roueché

Fiction

Black Weather
The Last Enemy
Feral
Fago

Nonfiction

Eleven Blue Men
The Incurable Wound
The Delectable Mountains
A Man Named Hoffman
The Neutral Spirit
What's Left
The Orange Man

FAGO

Berton Roueché

HARPER & ROW, PUBLISHERS

New York, Hagerstown, San Francisco, London

A HARPER NOVEL OF SUSPENSE

FAGO. Copyright © 1977 by Berton Roueché. All rights reserved. Printed in the United States of America. No part of this book may be used or reproduced in any manner whatsoever without written permission except in the case of brief quotations embodied in critical articles and reviews. For information address Harper & Row, Publishers, Inc., 10 East 53rd Street, New York, N.Y. 10022. Published simultaneously in Canada by Fitzhenry & Whiteside Limited, Toronto.

FIRST EDITION

Designed by Stephanie Krasnow

Library of Congress Cataloging in Publication Data

Roueché, Berton, date
    Fago.
    I. Title.
PZ3.R753Fag   [PS3535.0845]   813′.5′4   77–3804
ISBN 0–06–013689–8

77 78 79 80 10 9 8 7 6 5 4 3 2 1

This is a work of fiction. The setting is real—more or less—but the people are entirely imaginary.

Well may he smell fire, whose gown burns.

—GEORGE HERBERT,
Jacula Prudentum (1651)

ONE

1

Arlene came out on the back steps. She would have been at the kitchen window, watching me wade ashore. She stood there for a moment, featureless and strangely golden-haired in the sun, until she was sure I had seen her, and then raised her hand and waved. Come to lunch. I waved back. Clamming, even just for the table, is work, hard work, for a man of my age, and I was hungry. I took a last drag on my cigarette and ground it out in the pebbly sand at the edge of the pond. Back home, down in Missouri, we would have called it a lake, but here on the oceanic East End of Long Island anything much smaller than the ocean itself was a pond. That was one thing I had learned in a year and a half. The other thing was that there is nothing cheap (except clams, if you dig them yourself) about living in the country. Arlene had gone back in the house. I picked up my rake and the pail of clams and stumped up the slope to the meadow in the dead weight of my waders. A shadow moved across the faded meadow grass. I looked up: a crow. It was a bad-luck loner crow. I remembered the war, my war, and the Persian Gulf Command. The desert locals felt the same way about a solitary raven, and they had an exorcism. I watched the crow flapping alone across the spread of our meadow, over the hedgerow, over the roof of the Talmadge house, and into the dark of the woods beyond. A crow was only a smaller raven. I said aloud: "Raven, seek thy brother!" I smiled when I said it. But I meant it.

▲ ◢

I looked across the table. Arlene was sitting with her head down. She seemed to be staring into her coffee cup. She moved. She broke off a corner of toast and buttered it. She dropped it back on her plate.

I said: "What's the matter?"

She looked up. She shook her head. "Nothing," she said.

"There's something," I said. "What is it?"

"It really isn't anything," she said. "I just feel kind of blue." She took a little sip of coffee. "I dreamed about Charlie last night."

"Oh?" I said.

"It isn't anything," she said. "I'll be all right."

▲ ◢

I walked down to the road and opened the box and got out the mail. I sorted it out on the way back up to the house. *The New Yorker.* A solicitation from Common Cause. An overdue-book notice from the East Hampton Free Library. My retirement check. A bill from Mobil. A bill from Larry's Refuse Removal. A bill from Gristede's. A bill from White's Drug Store. I crumpled Common Cause and tossed it into the fireplace, and dropped the library card, the check, and the bills on the coffee table. I looked at them lying there: four bills and one check.

Arlene called down from the top of the stairs: "Any mail?"

"Not really," I said. *"The New Yorker* came. I got my check. Some bills."

I sat down with *The New Yorker.* I stared at the usual Tiffany ad and the usual incredible Steuben glass—an eight-inch contortion of crystal for sixteen hundred dollars. I went through the cartoons, and felt a little better. I turned back through the Cadillacs and the Porsches, the Chivas Regals and the Countess Maras, back through the vacations in Greece and Bermuda, to the "Talk of the Town." I read an account of a party, some kind of gathering, in a loft in SoHo, but I hardly knew what I was reading. I didn't even feel like reading. I got up and walked over to the front window and looked out at the empty road, the empty field, and the empty sky beyond. Upstairs, in the other bedroom, in Arlene's sewing room, the sewing machine droned and stopped and droned again. Arlene was right. Retirement was like a life sentence; it *was* a life sentence. It meant that

15

nothing now would ever change—at least not for the better. The only hope was a pardon, and that wasn't much of a hope. Because the only pardon was money.

▲◀

"You go on," I said. "I just want to . . ."

Arlene sat down on the arm of my chair. She took my face in her hands and gave me a savage kiss.

"I'll be up in a couple of minutes," I said.

She moved off the chair arm. She took a step, and turned back.

"Chick?"

"What?"

"Chick," she said. "It isn't a question of right or wrong. There's no such question anymore. It's just talk. The only question is this—what if we don't at least try? What else is there for us?"

"I'll be up in a couple of minutes," I said.

"I know," she said. "I understand. But I want you to understand something, too. I'm not going to give up and go on like this. I don't have that many years left. I'm tired of scrimping and slaving. Look at my hands! I want something more."

I sat on alone in the living room. I told myself she couldn't be serious. I told myself I couldn't take her seriously. I heard her come out of the bedroom and cross the hall to the bathroom. I told myself it was unthinkable. It was impossible. I heard the water running. Only, of course, it wasn't impossible. It was un-

16

thinkable, but it was possible. It was only too possible. I heard the toilet flush. I felt sick and frightened—the thought alone was frightening. It had to be frightening. But it was still there. It was still a thought, an idea. It was still a possibility.

Arlene came out of the bathroom.

"Chick?"

I got up and turned off the light.

"I'm coming," I said, and felt my way across the room in the dark.

2

I heard the car in the driveway, huffing up through the ruts, and went to the kitchen door. Arlene came out of the garage with a bag of groceries in her arms. I opened the screen and stepped out on the back porch.

"Can I help?"

"Ummm," she said. "There's another bag. And some stuff from the cleaners. And a bottle of wine."

"Wine?"

"Château something-or-other," she said. Her face was flushed. She looked excited. "Mr. England recommended it. He said it was very good."

"O.K.," I said. "But how come?"

I held the screen to let her through.

"To celebrate," she said. "Go get the rest of the stuff, and I'll tell you."

The other bag was half the size of the first. The stuff from the cleaners was my hound's-tooth jacket (three years old and the last of my Brooks Brothers clothes) and a skirt on hangers. I stuck the bottle under my arm, and bumped the car door shut with my rump. Arlene was waiting on the porch. She followed me through to the kitchen, and took the wine and the groceries. I hung the skirt and jacket on the knob of the closet door. I slipped the wine out of its paper bag. It was a good Bordeaux, a Pauillac of the Haute-Médoc. A few years ago, when we still had the apartment in New York, when I was still a senior research executive at Lambert Tucker Associates, when price was still no particular object, you could get it for under two dollars a bottle. I could imagine what it cost today. I put the bottle carefully back on the table.

"It looks good," I said. "But what are we celebrating?"

Arlene looked at me across the table.

"Chick," she said. She took a deep breath. "I think I've found him."

I said: "What do you mean?"

"Chick!" she said. "You know very well what I mean. I mean I think I've found our man."

I didn't say anything. I couldn't.

She said: "It was right on Newtown Lane. He was standing out in front of that terrible place next door to the shoe repair. The Wampum, or whatever they call it."

"The Wigwam."

"Yes," she said. "It was fantastic. It was just unbelievable. He was the right size, Chick. And the right age. And the right hair—except maybe his sideburns. I stopped and pretended to look in the shoe repair window, and I got a really good look. And he was a little strange. There was something sort of strange about him. Which was lucky. Because it gave me an excuse to ask Mrs. Golden at the cleaners. She didn't know much, but she told me his name. It's Fago—Ed Fago."

"Fago?" I said. "That doesn't sound very local."

"He isn't local," she said. "That's what makes him so right. He isn't anything. He isn't even married."

I felt a shiver, almost a chill, almost an adrenaline rush. But it didn't feel like fear. It was quicker, keener than that. It was an eagerness, an excitement.

"Yes," I said. "Yes—I see what you mean."

Arlene came around the table. She put her arms around me. She buried her face in my chest. I couldn't tell if she was laughing or crying.

▲ ◀

I put on my glasses and opened the telephone book— the big, floppy Suffolk County directory. Arlene stood looking over my shoulder. I found the *F*'s, and found the page, and started down the almost microscopic column. Fagan. A dozen Fagans. Fagelbaum. Fagelson. Fagerlund. Faggliani. Fagnet. Then Fagone. There was no Fago.

I closed the book and put it back on the shelf. I took off my glasses.

"Well," I said.

Arlene said: "I thought everybody had a telephone."

"Apparently not," I said. "Unless we've got the wrong spelling."

Arlene shook her head. "No," she said. "There isn't any other spelling."

"Maybe not," I said. "But let's make sure."

I turned back to the shelf and took out the other book —the bigger, floppier Manhattan directory. I got my glasses out again, and found the Manhattan *F*'s, and then the Manhattan Faganas. Then the Faganos. Then the Fagens. Then the Fagins. Then Faglio. Then— Fago. There was Fago Al Studios. There was Fago N. There was Fago Robert. I closed the book and put it away with the other.

"I guess you're right," I said.

Arlene stood there. She gave her head a violent shake. She said: "Damn him! I never heard of anybody without a telephone."

"It doesn't matter," I said. "We'll find him."

"I know we will," she said. "He's here—he lives here. But how?"

"We'll think of something."

Arlene said: "That didn't take very long."

She lay stretched out in the bathtub with the scented blue water up to her neck, and only her head, her breasts, and her knees afloat. She didn't look like a girl anymore, but she certainly didn't look fifty. I sat down on the toilet seat.

"I didn't see Parrot," I said. "He was home sick or something. I saw a new doctor named Chandler and I only had to wait a couple of minutes." I looked down at her, smiling up at me from her Caribbean bath. "He seems to be very well organized."

"Tell me."

"I think it went off pretty well," I said. "I mean, he didn't seem to be any more than just normally interested. I'm sure of that. He asked me what seemed to be the trouble, and I said I didn't exactly know. I said it the way we decided—I was vague, but I acted worried. I said I just didn't feel right. I said I was waking up early, at four or five o'clock, and couldn't get back to sleep. I said I didn't seem to have much appetite. I said I didn't feel exactly depressed, but I felt sort of dull and apathetic. I said I'd always been a great reader, but I'd sort of lost interest—I couldn't seem to concentrate anymore. And I said I didn't seem to have any energy. I felt tired all the time. O.K.?"

"Go on."

"I thought he was sympathetic," I said. "He didn't say much, but he seemed to really listen. I got the feeling he probably sees a lot of the same sort of thing. He didn't give it any name. He just said it wasn't uncommon in situations like mine. He had my folder there with my age and everything. He said it was probably a temporary reaction. He checked my blood pressure. He checked my heart. He asked some questions about drinking and exercise. I told him the truth—more or less. He said one thing that bothered me for a moment. I mean, I wasn't prepared. He asked about sex—my sex life."

"Oh?"

"He wanted to know if there had been any changes there. Was I apathetic about that, too? Had I lost the urge?"

Arlene smiled. And then looked serious. "What did you say?"

"Don't worry," I said. "I said yes. I said I didn't have much interest in anything. And it was the right answer. I could tell. It was the answer he expected."

"Yes."

"Well, that was about it. He talked about developing some new interests—hobbies, civic affairs, that kind of thing. I said I'd try. I said I had thought about doing some gunning later on. Some ducking, or pheasant-hunting. I said I used to shoot a little."

Arlene nodded. "Good," she said. "Very good."

"Yes," I said. "I thought so, too. And then he gave me a prescription for something called Elavil. The pharmacist at White's said it's what they call a mood elevator."

"That's perfect," she said. "That's just perfect."

"It seems an awful waste," I said. "I hate to tell you what it cost."

"Don't be silly," she said. "It might make all the difference." She sat up in a lurch of long white breasts and a splash of tinted water. "Hand me my towel."

"Dr. Chandler wants to see me again in a month."

"That's interesting," she said. "But I don't know." She took the towel. "We'll have to see."

"I see," I said. "Well, thanks very much."

I hung up.

Arlene said: "No?"

"No," I said. "They've never heard of him, either."

"Damn him," Arlene said. "I'm beginning to hate that man."

I looked at her, but she wasn't joking. Her face was tight and I knew that face. She meant it.

"You told me Mrs. Golden said he wasn't local," I said. "Maybe he doesn't . . ."

"No," she said. "He isn't local. He's from away. But he lives here."

"O.K.," I said. "Let's try Amagansett."

"All right."

I opened the directory again and turned the pages and found the number. I read it off. Arlene picked up the telephone, and dialed. She wet her lips and smiled, like an actress waiting ready in the wings.

I heard the scratch of a voice.

The actress had her cue. She said in a lofty voice: "The postmaster, please. Mr. George Derring calling."

There was another scratch, and she handed me the phone.

"Mr. Postmaster?" I said. I used my clearest Eastern Seaboard voice. "This is George Derring of Miles, Wickham, Tannhauser, and Poole, in Huntington. We have a little probate problem. We're trying to locate a party who may reside in your district."

"Yes, sir?"

"The name is Fago—*F-a-g-o.* E. Fago."

"Fago?" he said. "Would that be Edwin Fago?"

My heart gave a little jump. "That's right," I said. "Edwin Fago."

"Yes, sir," he said. "Mr. Edwin Fago is one of our customers."

"Good," I said. "That's splendid." I looked at Arlene, and nodded. "And may I have his address?"

"I'm sorry, sir," he said. "We don't keep that information. We don't have a delivery service in this district. Our customers call here at the post office for their mail."

"Oh," I said.

"Yes, sir," he said. "This is a small district, you know. But I can get mail to Mr. Fago. Just address your letter to this post office. The zip code is 11930."

"Oh," I said. I had to make an effort to go on. "Oh, I see. Well, thank you very much."

"Not at all," he said, and hung up.

I stood for a moment with the sound of space and emptiness whispering in my ear. I put the telephone back in its cradle.

"What's the matter?" Arlene said. "What happened? I thought . . ."

I told her.

She stood blank and silent. Then she gave a little shrug, and smiled.

She said: "But he does live in Amagansett?"

25

"Yes."

"And he has to go over to the post office there to get his mail?"

I nodded.

"So he probably goes there every day."

"Probably."

"I wonder when," she said. "There must be a regular time. I mean, when the mail is ready."

"I suppose we could find out," I said. "I don't suppose it's much of a secret."

▲◄

I was in the kitchen fixing us a drink when the telephone rang. It rang twice, and then I heard Arlene's answering voice. I went on with our drinks—Scotch for Arlene, bourbon for me. I could hear Arlene talking, but I couldn't hear what she said. I put the ice tray back in the refrigerator and gathered up the drinks and carried them back to the living room.

Arlene was still on the phone.

"I know," she was saying. "I know." She was wearing her smiling, cocktail party, telephone face. "And we'll miss you."

She hung up. Her smile slipped into a thoughtful look. She came back to her chair and sat down and took a good swallow of her drink.

"That was Gloria," she said. "This is their last weekend. They're closing their house on Sunday. They wanted us to have dinner on Saturday."

"Oh?"

"I really would like to go," she said. "We haven't done anything for ages."

"You didn't say yes?"

"Of course not."

"What did you say?"

"I said I thought they were good enough friends to hear the simple truth. I said we just weren't going out right now. I said you were just feeling too down. I said they would hardly know you these days. You didn't have any interest in anybody or anything. You were taking something called Elavil, but I didn't think it was doing much good. But I said you seemed to like Dr. Chandler. Gloria said she understood and everything. She was really terribly sweet."

Arlene picked up her drink and took a sip. She looked at me across the glass. And smiled.

"I said we'd see them in the spring," she said.

The Amagansett Post Office shared a block-long parking lot with an IGA, a liquor store, a Laundromat, and a gourmet shop, now closed for the season. A sign in its leaded-glass bow window read: "See You in April!" I parked at the post office end of the lot, between a Chevelle Malibu sedan and an International pickup truck. There wasn't a Mercedes, a BMW, an Alfa Romeo, or even a Volvo in sight. The season was definitely over.

Arlene handed me the letter. It was a bill—our bimonthly return to the Long Island Lighting Company, with its truculent admonition on the envelope: "Put stamp here. The Post Office will not deliver mail without postage." I was one of those who hadn't known they would, until it was too late. I stuck the envelope in my raincoat pocket, and got out in a misty drizzle. A narrow walk, flanked by barberry bushes strewn with cigarette butts, led up to the door. I went in and through a cluster of old men and middle-aged women and three or four business types. And up to the counter. I waited my turn beside a grim-faced woman bristling with pink plastic curlers. The postmaster brought her a shoebox package that smelled like something to eat. He looked nothing like the voice I had spoken to on the telephone. He was small and thin and bent and bald. He had to tilt up his head to look at me.

I bought a book of stamps, and put one on the envelope.

"Nasty day," I said.

"Yes, sir," he said. "We need it, though."

I nodded toward the crowd at the front of the room. "You always have a crowd like this? Or is it just the weather?"

He straightened, and craned his neck.

"Well," he said. "I guess the weather helps. But we always get a crowd at mail time—morning and afternoon, both."

"Oh?" I said. I didn't like that much. "You get two deliveries here?"

"Yes, sir," he said. "We get two deliveries and we

28

make two distributions. The morning mail is just about all out now. Our afternoon distribution is usually ready around four or four-thirty."

"So everybody comes in twice a day?" I said.

"Some do," he said. "And some don't. I guess it depends on if they're expecting something."

"I see what you mean," I said.

"Yes, sir," he said. His eyes shifted away, and down a couple of inches. "Morning, Fred," he said. "Looks like we might get our rain."

I dropped my bill in the slot, and went back up the room, and out. It was really raining now. I ran for the car.

Arlene sat huddled in her corner. The radio was shrilling with teen-age voices. She sat up, and turned it off.

"Well?"

"It isn't going to be easy," I said. "They distribute mail in the morning. And again in the late afternoon."

Mr. England arranged the bottles in a tight little row along the counter. He was a smiling man with smooth gray hair and a youthful black mustache. He gave the bottles a friendly look.

"Now, let's see," he said. "One Jim Beam. One John Begg. And one Gordon's vodka." He positioned himself at his calculator. He tapped the keys. He stepped back and consulted a chart on the counter. He tapped the keys again, and tore off a protruding slip of paper. He held the paper at arm's length. "That will be exactly eighteen dollars and seventy-six cents. With tax."

"I want to give you a check for that," I said.

"Oh, surely," he said. "Of course, Mr. Hill."

"And I'd like to have some cash," I said. "Could I add, say, fifty dollars to that?"

"Oh, surely," he said. "Be glad to."

I wrote out the check and took the cash and picked up the bag of bottles. Mr. England stood at attention behind the counter and watched me pass in review.

"Have a nice day," he said.

I stowed the bag in the back of the car with the bag from Amagansett Wines & Spirits and the bag from Silver's Discount Liquors. I had enough. I had as much as I dared for now. I drove out through the Robert C. Reutershan Memorial Parking Lot. I passed the Wigwam. It looked open but empty. Eleven o'clock in the morning was probably a little early even for its clientele. I turned down North Main Street, cut under the railroad trestle, and headed for home.

It took me two trips to get the three bags into the house. Arlene came in from somewhere as I was lining the bottles up on the kitchen table. They made an impressive display.

"My God!" she said.

"I agree," I said.

"We'll have to start having a drink before lunch," she said. "I hope it was worth it."

"It was," I said.

I reached in my pocket and brought out a gambler's roll of twenties, tens, and fives.

"How much?"

"A hundred and sixty," I said.

I opened the second drawer below the drainboard, and felt under the store of dish towels. I found the big manila envelope, and added my bills to the bills already there. They brought the total up to nearly seven hundred.

We sat in the car in the parking lot at the Amagansett Post Office with the windows up against the late-afternoon chill and watched the flow of old men in hunting caps and middle-aged women in buttoned sweaters and high school boys and girls in work clothes and once in a while a businessman in a suit and necktie. They went quickly, eagerly up the walk and in, and came slowly out, head down, reading as they came. After three days, I was beginning to know many of them by sight. I wondered if any of them had more than noticed us.

I shifted in my seat and tried to stretch my legs, and lighted a cigarette. I blew a long stream of smoke at the windshield.

Arlene turned her head. "That's your third cigarette since we've been here."

"Is it?" I said. "O.K."

I rolled down the window and threw it out. I looked at my watch. It was twenty minutes after four.

"It's almost four-thirty," I said.

She nodded. Then she said: "I wonder if maybe we ought to try coming in the morning instead."

"We can if you want to," I said. "But I don't know—I can't see him coming here at ten o'clock in the morning. He must work. He must have some kind of a job."

"I guess you're right."

"Maybe he's been sick," I said. "Or away. Or maybe he just doesn't get that much mail." I put my hand on her knee. I moved it up the swell of her thigh. "Don't worry. We'll find him."

"I'm not worried," she said. She put her hand on mine, and squeezed. "But I guess we might as well go."

"I'm ready," I said, and started the car.

I backed out and around, and headed out to the highway. I waited for a truck to go by. Then a car. Then another car.

Arlene gave a strangled sound, and sat straight.

She said: *"Chick!* Chick—that's him. That's him in that yellow car."

"Fago?"

"Yes—in that yellow car."

There was still another car coming, but I thought there was time enough. I swung into the highway and stamped hard on the accelerator, and followed. But I needn't have hurried. The truck up ahead was setting a cautious pace. I pulled up a length or two behind the yellow car. It was an old Dodge Dart, four or five years old, a four-door sedan, with the rear bumper broken and wired together and the right rear fender dented

32

and crusted with rust. I couldn't see much of the driver —the back of his head and a green stocking cap.

"I can't believe it," Arlene said. She was sitting on the edge of her seat with her eyes wide and her hands clenched in her lap. "It's so crazy. We sit there and wait and wait and then all of a sudden . . ."

"It's weird," I said.

We moved sedately along the highway and into the village and down the wide Main Street with the truck leading the way and a gathering parade behind. We passed the big brick New Deal school and the little white Catholic church and the row of antique shops and the Mobil station. The brake lights flashed on the yellow car, and then the left-turn blinker. He cut through a hole in oncoming traffic and nosed into the parking lot in front of Rudy's Diner & Cocktail Lounge. I braked, braked hard, and pulled off to the right and parked. I was a little shaken. I cut the engine.

"Well!" I said.

The driver's door on the yellow car came open. Fago got out. I rolled down my window for a better view. Arlene slid over beside me.

"Look at him, Chick," she said. "Look at him. You see what I mean?"

I looked. He looked to be about my height and build, but that was almost all I could tell from across the street in the fading light. We watched him come around his car and across the parking lot. He had on a dark red Windbreaker. He walked with a slouching stoop. He went stooping into the diner.

"Well?" she said.

"Yes," I said. "I guess you're right. But it's hard for me to say."

"He's perfect," she said.

I sat back. I started to reach for a cigarette. I thought again, and didn't.

"Now what?" I said. "It seems a little early for dinner. You don't suppose he works there?"

"No," she said. "He's not the type. And I don't think he's in the diner. You remember where I first saw him —outside that Wampum place. I think he's in the cocktail lounge."

"Oh, God," I said. "I hope not. He could be there all night."

"Then so will we," she said. "We're not going to lose him now."

She sat tense for a moment, and then turned on the radio. She found the twenty-four-hour Muzak station in Sag Harbor, and tuned it low. We sat there in an endless enveloping purr and watched and waited.

Rudy's was the Amagansett equivalent of the Wigwam. There were half a dozen cars and trucks parked in its parking lot. One of them had a bumper sticker that read: "Eat Clams and Live Longer/Eat Oysters and Love Longer." The diner door opened and a heavy-set couple came out. The man stumbled, and the woman caught his arm. He knocked her hand away savagely. They got in a new pale-green Chevrolet pickup truck, and the woman took the wheel. They

34

drove off toward East Hampton in a spindrift of gravel. It was full dusk now, almost dark.

I looked at my watch. It was twenty-five minutes to six.

I said: "What if I went in and took a look?"

"I don't think so," Arlene said.

"I could be buying a pack of cigarettes."

"No."

A car turned in and parked where the pickup truck had been. A man got out, a young man with chin whiskers. In the glare of the parking lot lights, his face looked vaguely familiar. I tried to place him.

Arlene touched my arm.

She said softly, secretively, in almost a whisper: "Here he comes."

Fago came down the steps, lighting a cigarette. He dropped the match and slumped on to his car.

I started the engine, and waited. The lights came on in the yellow car. It backed out and around and nosed slowly toward the street. It was impossible to tell which way he would go. I waited, watching his lights.

"Chick!"

"I see him."

The yellow car gave a forward lurch. It hesitated, then swung to the right, back toward the Amagansett Post Office, back the way it had come. And I was headed the other way. I pulled out to turn and follow. Two motorcycles, snarling and popping, went racing past in tandem. I slowed and waited, and then moved out and into my lane. I tried for the turn, and couldn't. I had to let a car full of yelling kids go by.

"Chick! Don't let him . . ."

I didn't answer. I hardly heard her. The street was clear behind me. I wrenched the wheel around, I made my U-turn, and came up fast behind the yelling kids. I hung as close as I dared on their tail, looking for a chance to pass. The yellow car was just ahead of the kids. I couldn't see it, but I knew it was there. I could see the spread of its lights.

There was a flash of red lights. It went off in my face like a bomb. The lights flashed and blazed, and the kids' car stopped—skidded and swerved and stopped. I had to stand on my brakes. Arlene screamed. I slid and gripped, and stopped clear of the kids' stopped car by no more than a foot. A door opened on the right side, and two kids—a boy and a girl—got waving and yelling out. The car moved on with a sudden jump. It slowed and stopped again and turned off to the left, off into Windmill Lane.

I cut around it on the right, gathering speed, moving fast, closing in on the car ahead. Then I was close enough. I didn't want to get too close. It moved into the sweep of the Main Street lights. But it wasn't the yellow car. There was no yellow car. The yellow car had turned off to the right or turned off to the left or had somehow vanished somewhere up the long length of Main Street. The car just ahead was a silvery blue Plymouth station wagon.

Arlene went over to the refrigerator. She took something out of the chest and walked back to the counter. She stood there with her back to me.

"I'm sorry," she said. "I didn't mean it that way. It wasn't your fault. I know that."

"All right," I said.

She turned and looked at me. "I mean it, Chick."

"O.K.," I said. "Are we going to have a drink?"

"I'd love a drink," she said. "In a minute. In a couple of minutes."

"O.K.," I said. "You let me know when."

I looked around. There was nothing I could do in the kitchen but stand there. I went out and through to the living room, and sat down. I picked up Arlene's *House & Garden*—and put it down again. There was this morning's *Times*. But I had finished with that before lunch. There was yesterday's *Star*—yesterday's weekly East Hampton *Star*. I picked it up and stared at the front page. I moved on—through the obituaries, through the weddings and engagements, through the local political columns. I stopped at an eerie photograph of moonrise on the ocean beach. I glanced down the page, and a headline caught my eye: "Another Brawl at the Wigwam." I read on:

The East Hampton Village Police Department made three arrests last week, and was called upon to investigate an alleged burglary. Two of the arrests grew out of a brawl, the fifth this year, at the Wigwam Tavern on Newtown Lane early Sunday morning. Harlan K. Trooper, 51, of 30 Lester Street, East Hampton, and Edwin Fago, 59, of Cedar Pond Road, Amagansett, were charged with disturbing the peace. Both pleaded guilty in Town Justice Court on Monday and were released upon payment of fines of $25 each. According to police, the third arrest . . .

I put the paper back on the table and got up and went back to the kitchen. My heart was jumping and my chest felt tight. Arlene heard me coming, and looked up.

"Oh, Chick," she said. "I was just going to . . ."

I said: "Have you ever heard of a road in Amagansett called Cedar Pond Road?"

"Cedar Pond Road?" she said. "I don't think so. Why?"

"Because that's where Ed Fago lives," I said. "He lives on Cedar Pond Road."

3

I drove down the wide, empty Sunday-morning street
with the imitation-parchment map of East Hampton
Town from Things n' Stuff folded open to Amagansett
on the seat beside me. It was perfectly, almost eerily,
still. The shades were drawn at the bedroom windows
of all the houses I passed. This was the deadest hour of
the week. It was several hours too late for Rudy's and
it was still too early for church. Even the big Mobil
station was closed.

I slowed just short of the fire station, and looked again
at the ridiculous map. Cedar Pond Road was a narrow,
potholed blacktop that I had always supposed was a
private road or a driveway. It cut inland from Main
Street between two towering thickets of privet, it ran
between a forgotten apple orchard and a fallen-down
barn, it emerged between two endless potato fields, it
climbed the slope of Egypt Ridge. Then the woods
began. I passed the scar of a gravel pit. I passed a peeling white clapboard house with a washing machine on
the front porch. A homemade sign nailed to a big oak

tree read: "Bud Chase." The heavy woods closed in again. I caught a glint of steely water through a screen of trees on the right. Some of the trees were cedars. A clearing appeared, and a row of three darkly weathered, shingle-sided houses came into view. One of the houses had a sign out front: "Lipton." Two of the houses had thirty-foot television antennas rising from the roof, and there was a car in every driveway—a green Ford pickup truck, a tan Volkswagen van, a black Oldsmobile sedan. There was an old International Scout pulled up on the grass in front of the Lipton house. I drove on.

The road took a sudden turn, and dropped down a long, thickly wooded hill. There was a patch of weedy meadow at the foot of the hill. There was another shingle-sided house—a little one-story house with a dogleg stovepipe thrusting out and up from a window—at the far end of the meadow. There was a rutted dirt driveway just beyond the house. And there was a car in the driveway—a yellow Dodge Dart, an old sedan, with a broken rear bumper and a dented right rear fender. It was parked askew and the driver's door was hanging open.

I drove past the house, out of sight of the house, and stopped. I picked up the map and worked out where I was. Cedar Pond Road ended at a junction with another ridge road called Cross Highway. Cross Highway connected with the Old Springs Road. I knew the Old Springs Road. I could get home from there. I turned on the radio, and drove off to the screaming excitement of a back-to-the-Bible Church of Holiness choir.

I pushed the lawnmower away. I had to get rid of it, I had to hide it, I couldn't stand to look at it. I began to shiver, to tremble—and woke up. I was still shaking. And then I realized. It was Arlene shaking me.

"Chick!"

I could feel her warmth, her softness. I opened my eyes to the dark. But it was the familiar dark of the bedroom. I was safe. It hadn't happened.

"Chick—are you all right?"

"What's the matter?"

"You were moaning. I thought there was something wrong. It frightened me."

"I guess I was . . ." But the dream was already beginning to dim and change and drift away. I said: "I was cutting the grass. I dreamed I was cutting the grass. And I ran over a toad. I think it was a toad. The mower —I don't know. There was something about it. It was horrible."

Arlene said: "A toad!" I heard her catch her breath. "That's kind of weird. I mean, it's really strange. Don't you remember, Chick? I killed a toad last summer. Only it wasn't the mower. It was the hoe. I was weeding the garden. Don't you remember?"

Fago came slumping around the side of the house. I watched him from the shadowed shelter of a fringe of woods across the road. He stopped and looked up at the heavy early-morning sky and stretched. He blew his nose between thumb and finger, and wiped it on his sleeve. He walked around the open door of his car and went on to the rear and dropped down on his knees. I was too far away to make out what he was doing. He got up and went back around the side of the house. I glanced down the road. I had left my car backed in behind a curtain of creeper and scrub at the mouth of a rut-track trail. It was visible but inconspicuous.

I heard a creak and a rattle. Fago reappeared, hunched and huffing, pulling what looked like a two-wheeled cart. It was a homemade trailer with a wide, flat bed and four high sides made of chicken-wire fencing. He dragged the trailer around to the rear of his car, and fixed it to a hitch. He looked up again at the dismal sky, and then got in his car and slammed the door. He had to slam it twice. The engine raced and roared. I edged away through the trees, and broke for my car. I slid behind the wheel, and craned my neck to see. Fago backed charging out of the driveway, and swung around. He headed toward Amagansett. I watched him charge off in a pluming smog of burning oil, the trailer skipping and skittering behind. When he was halfway up the hill, I started the engine and followed.

I followed him into Amagansett village. I followed him down the long Main Street. He was easy to follow with his rattletrap trailer, and I let him keep a block or more ahead. I followed him on to East Hampton. I followed him out the long Main Street of East Hampton. I followed him around the Town Pond and the Town Green and the ancient burying ground. He turned into Ocean Avenue. The lawns spread, the shade trees soared, and the houses withdrew up circular graveled driveways. These were the estates of the sojourning rich. Fago turned into one of the gleaming driveways. And this was where Fago worked. I slowed and hung back, and then drove slowly past. A wrought-iron sign on wrought-iron legs read: "Hollister." Fago had parked in a service branch of the driveway, and he was standing alongside the trailer with a bamboo rake in his hand. Fago would never be seriously missed. Fago was a yardman.

▲◢

I drove on to the end of the road—to the "Dead End" sign and the empty plain of beach and the cold gray ocean beyond. I parked in the empty "Ambulance Zone: No Parking," and lighted a cigarette. I sat and smoked and looked at the ocean. It was hard to remember its sparkling blue August allure. I looked at my watch, and sat for another five minutes. But I had already made up my mind. It wasn't on the program, but it was something I had to do. One distant glimpse in Rudy's parking lot at dusk and the even more distant glimpse this morning were not enough. I had to know more than that. I had to really see. I turned and drove back to the Hollister place.

Fago was raking leaves in the skeletal shadow of a giant copper beech a few yards in from the road. I pulled up and slid over to the passenger's seat. I stuck my head out the window.

"Excuse me . . ."

Fago stopped raking. He slowly turned and looked. It was a peculiar, almost hangdog look.

He said: "Huh?"

I said in my commanding George Derring voice: "I'm afraid I need some help."

He dropped his rake on a pile of leaves on a spread-out square of gunnysacking, and came slumping over.

"Yeah?"

"I'm looking for a street called Cottage Avenue," I said. "I think it's around here somewhere."

Fago stood and looked at me. His eyes were blue, a pale, pale blue, the color almost of juniper berries. He seemed to be trying to think.

"Cottage Avenue?"

"That's right," I said. "They said it was around here somewhere."

"Well," he said. "This here is Ocean Avenue. What you want to do is . . ."

I stopped listening. I was seeing what Arlene had seen that day on Newtown Lane. I saw, and understood. Fago and I looked nothing alike. His nose was too

44

big, his ears were too small and flat, his eyes were too palely blue—there was no sort of resemblance. We shared only a size and build, an approximate age, a commonplace abundance of graying brown hair. We shared only what was needed—the essential silhouette. I felt a rush of relief. I wasn't looking at myself. I was seeing a total stranger.

▲ ◢

Arlene said: "I know. But I've been thinking. And I've changed my mind."

I took a last bite of bacon, a last bite of toast, a last swallow of coffee. I found my cigarettes and lighted one.

"You don't think it's risky?"

"There's always a risk," she said.

"I'm not too sure I can handle it a second time," I said. "I told you he really impressed me. I told you he's no fool. I could blow the whole thing."

She shook her head. "Chick," she said. "He asked you to come back in a month. He expects you to come back. Suppose you don't. That could really blow it. He'd write you off as a waste of time. You'd be just another hypochondriac—or worse. We want him on our side. He could be a vital witness. He could make all the difference. We don't want him against us."

"No," I said. "I understand that."

I sat for a minute. I knew she was right, but I didn't feel easy about it.

"I know all that," I said. "But how do I talk to him this time? What do I say?"

"We'll work it out," she said. "I have to go into the village this afternoon. I'll stop by the library again."

▲ ◀

Dr. Chandler sat back in his leather swivel chair. He wasn't much more than half my age, but his face was deeply lined and his hair was thin and already going gray. He gazed without expression at the assemblage of framed certificates on the wall above his desk—college, medical school, internship, residency, clinical professorship, American Academy of Family Physicians. My folder lay open before him. He rolled his pen between his palms.

He said: "Worse?"

"Well," I said. "I can't say I feel any better."

"I see," he said. He glanced down at my folder. "You were having some trouble sleeping. Do you think there's been any improvement there?"

"I don't have any trouble getting to sleep," I said. "My problem is staying asleep. I wake up and I start thinking—and I'm wide awake. I lie there sometimes till morning."

Dr. Chandler rolled his pen. "What do you think about?" he said.

46

I shrugged. "My life," I said. "My age. My finances. I think about the future—what's left of it. It isn't really thinking, I guess. You couldn't really call it that. It doesn't solve anything. It's more like—I don't know. Like dreading. Like despairing."

"Mmmm," he said. "And how do you feel in the morning?"

I hesitated. "Well," I said. "Night thoughts are always different, I guess. I don't feel quite so hopeless in the morning. But . . ."

"Yes," he said. "In the morning—would you say you wake up refreshed? Or not?"

"I haven't had a good night's sleep, a real night's sleep, in a long time," I said. "And I don't wake up in the morning. I'm already awake."

He nodded. "Mmmm," he said. "I had hoped . . ." He looked at my folder again. "You've been taking Elavil. Uh—seventy-five milligrams at bedtime?"

"Seventy-five milligrams?" I said. "I guess so. I mean, if that's what you prescribed."

"And you're still not sleeping," he said. "And your energy level is still low. And your appetite is still off. And your sex drive . . ." He gave his nose a gentle pull. "I would have hoped, I would have thought—but it's hard to know about the tricyclic compounds. Different people respond differently. I think we'll increase your Elavil a bit."

He opened a drawer and took out a prescription pad. I watched him writing. He seemed no more than professionally disappointed. I was sure it was no more than that. I let myself begin to relax. It couldn't be much longer now.

Dr. Chandler handed me the scribbled slip. He sat back in his chair. He began to roll his pen again.

"I've increased your dose by seventy-five milligrams," he said. "I want you to continue on as before with seventy-five milligrams at bedtime. We'll spread the increase through the day—twenty-five milligrams before each meal." He tossed his pen on the desk and watched it roll away. "Let's give this a couple of weeks. I'd like to see you again in—let's say three weeks. Then we'll see. My feeling is we'll begin to see some real improvement. If not—then we'll have to think about a new drug. Or, perhaps, a psychiatric consultation. There's a very good man in Southampton."

"I don't think I'd like that much," I said.

"No," he said. He smiled. "Neither would I."

The consultation seemed to be over.

"Well," I said, and started to get up.

He cleared his throat.

"Just one more thing," he said. His smile was gone. He gave me a long, grave look. It was more than grave. It was worried. "Tell me," he said. "Have you been having any bad thoughts? Have you had any thoughts of—suicide?"

I stood stiff and still. But I was tingling. I was churning. It was all I could do to return his uncomfortable look. I let a moment pass.

I said: "I—I guess it has occurred to me. I guess I've

48

thought about it. But I don't think I'd ever do a thing like that."

▶ ◀

I drove home in the rain with the taste of too many beers in my mouth, and my fingers smelled of too many cigarettes. I wasn't drunk—I didn't think I was drunk. I just felt heavy and full. I wasn't used to beer. I turned into the driveway. There was a seep of light at the bedroom windows. It was almost one o'clock, but Arlene was still awake, still up. I smiled, and my face felt stiff and brittle. Maybe I *was* a little drunk. I parked the car and felt my way back through the dark to the front of the garage. I stood there for a moment in the shelter of the overhang, listening to the pelt of rain and breathing the frosty fresh smell of the night. Then I ducked my head and ran for the kitchen door. And in. And through the dining room.

"Chick—is that you, Chick?"

"It's me."

I belched, and went up the stairs, holding the rail, and along the hall. Arlene was sitting up in bed in her flowered robe with an empty glass of something on the table beside her and a copy of *The New Yorker* open on her lap. I sat down on the edge of the bed. She smiled and held out her arms, and I moved to kiss her.

She pulled abruptly back.

"Ugh!" she said. "Go away!"

"What's the matter?"

"You," she said. "You smell awful. You smell like a brewery."

"Oh?" I smiled my brittle smile. "I guess I do. But I thought their beer was safer than their whiskey."

"Who is 'they'—the Wampum?"

I shook my head. It felt as strange as my smile.

"I don't know who runs it," I said. "It's that dump on the way to the Town Dock. The Swamp Creek Tavern, they call it."

"And?"

"That's where I've been," I said. "I mean, that's where I ended up. That's where I finally found him."

"And?"

"I tried Rudy's first," I said. "But there were only a couple of cars there. I didn't even have to go in. Then I tried the Wigwam. He wasn't there, but I hung around for about an hour. I have a feeling that he doesn't go there anymore—not since that fight. Then I had a hunch and drove out to the Swamp Creek Tavern, and there he was."

"And?"

"Alone," I said. "He was alone. No girl, no particular friend—nothing. He sat at the bar the whole time I was there and he talked to the bartender and some of the guys around him, but mostly he just sat there and drank beer and smoked and watched the television. He doesn't have anybody close. He's a loner. I'm sure of that."

Arlene nodded. "It's fantastic," she said. "It's almost too good to be true. And I like the idea of the Swamp

50

Creek Tavern. I never liked the Wampum. It's too public there on Newtown Lane. But I like the Swamp Creek Tavern—I like it a lot. I think it's the perfect place, up there in the woods. It's the perfect location."

"I don't know if you remember," I said. "But there's a good-sized parking lot off to one side. It's maybe an acre. And there aren't any lights."

"It's just perfect."

"I think so, too," I said.

We sat for a moment, just looking at each other. I felt suddenly taut and out of breath. Arlene began to smile. I moved toward her again.

"No," she said.

But I heard the tremble in her voice, the familiar telltale stir. She closed *The New Yorker* and put it on the bedside table, and began to unbutton her robe.

"Go brush your teeth," she said. "And get out of those Swamp Creek clothes. And—and then come back."

▶▲

I dropped the yellow legal-size scratch pad on the kitchen table and pulled up the other chair and sat down. I took out my pen. And had a sudden thought. I looked at Arlene across the table.

"I wonder," I said. "I wonder if a pencil might be better."

"Why?"

"I don't know," I said. "Less formal, maybe. It might seem more spontaneous."

51

"I don't think it matters that much," she said. "I think they use whatever they usually use. I think you'd use your pen."

"That's the trouble," I said. "I just wish we had something to go by. There must be some kind of pattern. But the papers never give any details."

"I think there're probably dozens of patterns," she said. "I think everybody probably makes his own."

"May be," I said. "O.K." I looked down at the blank sheet of paper. It was like being back in the shop again. The beginnings were always the hardest part. I triggered my pen and scratched it a couple of times on the back of the pad to get a flow of ink. "Well—how do we start?"

"It's a letter," she said. "You're writing me a letter. So you start it the way you always do."

"Yes," I said. "But I don't mean that. I mean, how do I start off? What do I say?"

Arlene hesitated. "We'll just have to feel our way." She put her elbows on the table and rested her chin in her hands. "I think maybe some expression of regret. I think I've read that somewhere. Maybe there *is* a certain pattern; maybe it just evolves. Anyway, I think you begin by saying you're sorry."

"I think you're right," I said.

Arlene sat looking down at the spidery grain of the table. "Yes," she said. "You're sorry—but you're doing what you have to do; it's the only possible way."

"Yes," I said. I could feel it now. It was started, it was moving. "Yes—it's the only way out. But it's no fault of yours. You're not in any way to blame; you've been wonderful. It's all my fault. I can't go on. I've tried but I haven't the strength. I'm too old, it's too late. I'm worthless. I'm a burden."

Arlene raised her head.

"Chick," she said. "That's perfect. That's absolutely perfect." Her eyes were bright and shining. "You're sorry and you ask me to forgive you. Because I've done all that was humanly possible. Because I've been wonderful. I've been a perfectly wonderful wife."

I got stiffly up and went over and turned the television off. Brandon de Wilde gave one last, shattering, heartbroken cry of "Shane!"—and Alan Ladd blurred and shrank to a tiny pinpoint of light. The light went out. I went back to my chair, but I didn't, I couldn't, sit down. I looked at my watch. It was almost twelve, almost midnight. It was time.

Arlene stirred. "I don't think I want to see that ever again," she said.

I said: "I think we'd better get started."

"All right," she said. "But, Chick—try to relax. I don't like to see you so tense."

"I'm not tense," I said. "I'm just restless. I want to get started."

"I'm ready," she said.

We got our coats from the kitchen closet, and Arlene put on a big knitted cap. I went over to the counter, to the magnetic wall rack where Arlene kept her knives, and took the knife I wanted—a boning knife with a wooden handle and a six-inch stiletto blade. I found an old wine cork in the catchall drawer below and stuck it on the knife point. I dropped the knife in my pocket. Arlene was watching me from the door. She was smiling, but her face was closed. She opened the door and went through, and I followed her into the night.

Arlene drove. I sat silent beside her, feeling the strange shape of the blunted knife in my pocket. We had talked it out too many times, we had taken it as far as talk could take it, and there was nothing left to say. It was a black night, pitch black with a dense, dark-of-the-moon blackness that seemed to dim the headlights. The road ahead looked barely visible, and the lights of the occasional cars coming toward us had the look of lights in fog. We turned off the dim tunnel of the open county road and into the dimmer wooded tunnel of Aaron's Path. Aaron's Path led down to the water, down to the Town Dock, down to the Swamp Creek Tavern. I hunched down in my seat and tried not to think, tried not to anticipate.

Arlene made a doubtful sound. I took my eyes off the empty road. In the faint light of the dashboard I could see the edge of her profile, the set of her jaw.

I said: "What's the matter?"

"Nothing."

"I thought you said something."

"Not really—I was just thinking about the key to the cellar door."

"You asked me to check," I said. "I left the lock on the door. The key's on the nail on the porch."

Arlene nodded.

Then she said: "I see some lights. Is that it down there on the left?"

"That's it," I said.

▲ ◄

The Swamp Creek Tavern was a long, low building set close to the road at one end of a sandy clearing hacked out of the woods. It was built of cement blocks and painted a shiny bottle green. There was a convolution of neon in three of its four front windows—Budweiser, Miller High Life, Schmidt's. The fourth window was screened by a Venetian blind. These were the only lights. The parking lot was pretty well filled for early November. And Fago's car was there.

We circled the ruts and potholes of the parking lot and found his car almost where I had found it parked the Saturday night before, at the back of the lot, with only three or four cars between it and the blank, windowless side of the building. Arlene parked in the rank behind it and a couple of cars away. She cut the engine and turned off the lights. We sat there in the blinding dark, and the only sound was the tick of the cooling engine.

I heard Arlene move, the brush of her coat on the seat. I felt her hand on my knee, on my arm. She found my hand.

"I'm all right," I said.

She gave my hand a squeeze.

"I know you are," she said.

56

The natural night began to return. The total dark softened and shifted and drew back to the woods, to the cars, to the loom of the building. I watched the wall and a pitch of roof emerge, black against the mere dark of the sky. It was like a distant stir of dawn. It was suddenly light enough, or dark enough, to see. I had a jarring thought. I hesitated, and then opened the door.

Arlene said, whispered: "What are you doing?"

"I'll be back in a minute," I said. "I just want to check . . ."

I felt my way along and through the row of cars to what looked like the right silhouette. I groped and touched and recognized the dent of the fender, the wired-on broken bumper. I had my bearings now. I moved quickly around to the left, to the door behind the driver's seat, and tried the handle. The door came open easily. It wasn't locked; it wasn't jammed. I hadn't really thought it might be, but I had to be sure. I didn't want any last-minute surprises. I left the door ajar on the latch, and moved quickly back to our car. To sit. And think. And wait.

▲◂

I heard something. I rolled the window down another three or four inches and leaned into the cold and listened. It was louder now—a crunch, a scuffle of feet in sandy gravel. I took a shallow, listening breath. The footsteps crunched. The darkness changed, something darker than the darkness moved, and I saw him. He

57

came scuffling along between the rows—tall, hunched, and suddenly clearly Fago.

Arlene gripped my hand.

She said: "Chick?"

"I know," I said. I put my mouth to her ear. "Now don't be too quick to leave."

"No."

"Wait until you're sure I'm . . ."

"I will."

I eased the door carefully open. I got carefully out. Fago had reached his car. Just beyond the black bulk of the car I could see the hunch of his shoulders, the back of his neck, the point of his stocking cap. He seemed to be just standing there. I waited. Then I heard a little splash, a little trickle of running water. Fago was urinating. The trickle went on and on, and stopped, and started again, and slowly dribbled away. He stood for a moment, and hawked and spat. He stooped and opened the door. He ducked into the car. The lights went on. I heard the starter begin to grind. I moved as fast as I could with care.

Fago sat humped over the wheel, still grinding away at the starter. He didn't hear me coming. He didn't hear me open the door. He didn't hear me slide into the seat behind him. I felt in my pocket for the boning knife and got it out and thumbed off the protective cork. I waited until the engine came alive, roared, and gentled back to an idle. Then I reached over and closed the door. I slammed it. Fago gave a jump, and twisted around in his seat. I let him turn. I let him see me sitting there. I let him stare. I smiled and leaned forward and put the point of my knife just under his Adam's apple.

I said: "Hello, Ed."

His stare froze.

"Hey," he said. "Hey—what is this?"

He tried to swallow, and his Adam's apple nudged the knife point. He jerked violently back. I followed him. I put the knife on his neck again. He stopped, and sat where he was.

He said: "What—what is this?"

"I've got a message for you," I said.

"Huh?"

"You've got an appointment, Ed."

"Appointment?" he said. His eyes popped and his face sagged. "I don't get it. What is this?"

"He wants to see you, Ed."

He started to shake his head—and remembered. He sat stiff.

He said: "Jesus Christ—what is this? I don't know what you're talking about."

"No?" I said.

I put a little more pressure on the knife. I didn't draw blood. It was just enough to feel. He gave a little yell.

"No?" I said.

His eyes bulged. He said: "Listen! I mean, honest to God. This is crazy. There's got to be some mistake. I mean, you got the wrong guy."

"He doesn't make mistakes," I said. "You know that, Ed. Now—let's get going!"

"I swear to God . . ."

"You heard me, Ed—let's go!"

He jerked the car into motion. He backed, and turned, and stalled. The starter ground. We jerked abruptly off again. There was a flare of headlights behind us. I looked back. A car swung around the row, moving fast, kicking gravel. Arlene was on her way.

"All right, Ed," I said. I made myself comfortable on the seat behind him, and moved the knife an inch or two. I didn't want him to feel it, I didn't want to hurt him if we happened to hit a bump. I just wanted him to remember, to know it still was there. "Go out to the road, Ed—then turn to the right. Then go straight until I tell you when."

▶ ◀

Fago sat slumped on the edge of the canvas cot. He still wore his cap and his Windbreaker jacket, but he sat in his stocking feet. I had taken his shoes, his scuffed brown loafers, for safekeeping. But it really seemed hardly necessary. He had let me take them without a word. The fight, the fervor, had gone out of him. It was as if his Saturday night had suddenly, belatedly hit him. He looked only beerily fuddled.

"O.K., Ed," I said. "Just try to be patient. He'll see you first thing in the morning."

Fago raised his head. He stared, but he didn't say anything.

I reached up and unscrewed the bulb from the ceiling socket, and put it in my pocket. The last thing I saw as the cellar went dark was his heavy, sagging stare. I found the steep stone steps and went up and out and unhooked the double doors and dropped them closed and locked them with the padlock. That took care of Fago for the night. I felt my way around the side of the house to the back porch. Arlene was waiting at the kitchen door.

"Is he all right?" she said. "He's awfully quiet."

"He's all right," I said.

I pushed the light bulb into one of the loafers and the boning knife into the other, and stowed them out of the way behind the door until morning. Fago would probably be a very different man by then. But I didn't want to think about that now. This wasn't the end of our Saturday night. Our night had just begun. I looked at my watch. It was twenty minutes to two. I sat down at the kitchen table, and lighted a cigarette. I wasn't exactly tired; I was too wound up for that. I just felt drained for the moment, and I was sweating. I unbuttoned my raincoat.

Arlene stood looking at me.

She said: "Are *you* all right?"

"I could use a drink," I said.

She hesitated. "Are you sure you really . . . ?"

"I need a drink," I said.

"All right."

She got out a glass and ice and my bottle of Jim Beam. She fixed a drink, a good dark drink, and brought it over to the table. I took a good swallow.

"Aren't you going to have one?"

"I wouldn't dare," she said. "I'd be afraid."

I took another swallow. It made me feel almost ready again.

"Chick?"

"Mmmm?"

"What happened?" she said. "I mean, you haven't told me anything. Did it go all right?"

"It went fine," I said. "I'll tell you about it later. But right now . . ." I finished my drink and stood up. I had even stopped sweating. I buttoned up my coat.

I said: "I want a good head start. Let's say at least twenty minutes. I don't want you waiting out there on the road. I want to be waiting for *you*."

"I know," she said. "I'll take my time." She stood tense, her hands hugging her shoulders. "And, Chick?"

"What?"

"Don't forget the refrigerator."

▲ ◀

Fago's car had the feel of a truck. The wheel had a good five inches of play, and it drove with a list to the right that felt like a broken spring. I began to think I should have asked for a start of half an hour. But it moved, and I had the roads to myself. I passed one car on Cross Highway. Then nothing the rest of the way.

I turned into Fago's driveway. I drove on to the end, to the rickety rear of the chicken-wire trailer and the rise of a shed beyond. I sat for a moment to fix the position of the house in my mind, and then turned off the lights. I took the keys and got out and locked up the car. I knew that Fago usually left his car unlocked, but this was a different case. I stood getting my bearings in the sudden dark. From somewhere off across the open meadow came a feeble, wavering whistle. It came again —a screech owl. It was a sound that spoke the bottom of the night, and it gave me a little shiver. Then I followed the memory of my momentary glimpse of the place across to the back of the house and found and unlocked the door.

I stepped into a stuffy dry heat and a smell of fried onions and bacon grease. By the tiny flickering glow of a space heater sunk in the floor I found a switch and switched on a light in the ceiling. There was no need for caution yet. The car in the driveway was Fago's car. I looked around the room. There was a sink and a counter along one wall and a stool in front of the counter. There was a refrigerator and a gas stove. There was a little white plastic radio on a shelf. There was a plastic table and two chairs in a corner, with a sooty clam shell ashtray and a rumpled pile of East Hampton *Stars*. There was a hall on the other side of the room with an open bathroom door and a door that was probably a closet. A door beyond that would be the door to the bedroom. On a hunch, I went over and looked in the sink. It was a mess—three slimy plates, a black frying pan, a coffee cup with a clot of pale gray coffee, a knife, two spoons, and an egg-yolked fork. I looked around for some kind of soap and a towel. It was certain now that I was going to need every minute of that twenty-minute start.

I found a cupboard for the dishes and a drawer for the cutlery. The frying pan I left on the stove. I started for the bedroom. I remembered Arlene's reminder, and opened the refrigerator. There wasn't much, but it could have looked a little funny. Nobody leaves a refrigerator full of food. I cleaned out the stuff that looked wrong—three eggs, the remains of a pound of bacon, a stick of margarine, some gray ground meat in a plastic tray, a carton of milk, a quart bottle of beer. I poured the beer and the milk down the drain, and put the containers in a garbage can under the sink. I wrapped the rest in one of the *Stars* and left it on the counter. That finally took care of the kitchen. I went on to the bedroom.

Fago's bed was unmade. It didn't look as if he often bothered to make it. I straightened the sheet and blanket, and let it go at that. I found a big tan suitcase under the bed. The list that Arlene and I had drawn up stood clear in my mind. I started with clothes. I found a brown suit, a dusty coat and trousers, on a wire hanger. I found a raincoat. The only shoes were a pair of work shoes and a pair of heavy laced boots, and I left them there on the closet floor. I went through a chest of drawers, and packed underwear, socks, three shirts, a couple of handkerchiefs, and an imitation hand-painted necktie. There were no pajamas to pack. Fago apparently didn't bother with pajamas. I took my list into the bathroom. Fago hadn't bothered to flush the toilet. I flushed it for him, and spread out a towel on the top of the seat. I emptied the medicine cabinet into the towel —toothbrush, toothpaste, razor, razor blades, shaving cream, comb, a big bottle of aspirin, a bottle of Di-Gel, a bandoleer of Maalox tablets, a box of bicarbonate of soda, a package of Ex-Lax, a prescription bottle of blue and yellow capsules. That was the end of the list. I closed the suitcase and turned off the light and went back to the kitchen and got the package of food and turned off the kitchen light and went out and closed and locked the door.

The night seemed darker and windier and colder. It felt much colder. I took a couple of steps—and something made me think. I remembered. My heart gave a lurch of thanksgiving. I went back to the house and let myself in and turned on the light and got down on my knees and lifted the grille on the space heater and found the valve and turned the heater off. I locked the house up again and went around to the front. The road was empty. I had done it with time to spare. I put down the suitcase and waited. But my heart was still thumping.

There was no sound from the cellar room below. I hung our coats in the kitchen closet, and Arlene emptied my package of ground meat and bacon and eggs and margarine into the garbage can. She turned and gave me

65

a ghastly smile. I followed her through the house and up the stairs. Her back was bent and her hair hung lank. I felt the same way. Every step was like wading through knee-deep water. I shifted the suitcase to my other hand and looked at my watch. It was five minutes after three. It had been a heavy three hours.

I dragged myself into the guest room, into Arlene's sewing room, and shoved the suitcase under the bed. It took me three shoves to do it right. The adrenaline, if that's what it was, had finally given out. Arlene was running water in the bathroom. I didn't have the strength to even brush my teeth. It was all I could do to get out of my clothes. I left them every which way on the chair, and dropped into bed, and sank.

"Chick?"

I climbed back to a kind of consciousness.

"Ummm?"

"Chick—did you set the alarm?"

I managed to shake my head.

She said: "I'm tired, too, you know."

I managed to open my eyes. The clock was on my bedside table. Arlene's face loomed, and then drifted out of focus and away.

"All right," she said. "But what do you think—seven o'clock? You can't make it any later than that."

I made an effort and nodded. And sank again, beyond recall.

The alarm went off. It rang into a muddled dream. It was the doorbell, then the telephone. It rang on, and into reality. I sat up in the first gray dusk of dawn and turned on the light. I was suddenly fully awake. I was more than that: I was renewed, fully renewed. I wouldn't have believed it possible.

Arlene raised her head. She gave me a blank look, and fell back. I let her sleep. Her time would come later. I put on a clean pair of chinos and a clean blue denim shirt and a thick cable-knit sweater that went back to my skiing days. I gathered up my trousers and shirt of the day, or the night, before, and rolled them into a bundle and stuck it under my arm. A few more wrinkles wouldn't matter. I turned out the light for Arlene and went into the bathroom. But not to shave, not even to wash. There wasn't time for that. I was a known, established early riser. I had to be ready by eight o'clock at the latest. I opened the medicine cabinet and took down the bottle of Elavil and shook out my prescribed bedtime dose—three twenty-five-grain tablets. I hesitated. For good measure, I shook out another. Half of the rest I flushed down the toilet: the bottle mustn't look too full.

I put the tablets in my pocket and went down the stairs and back through the dark of the house to the kitchen. The kitchen was full of a thin, cold light, as cold and thin as moonlight. It was almost morning now. Through the window I could see the first bright glints of pink and silver spreading across the pond. I ran some water in the teakettle and put it on to boil. There was suddenly so much to do that I felt a pinch of panic. I opened the closet and got out the old shooting jacket I had been wearing all fall and made a new bundle of yesterday's shirt and trousers and Fago's old brown loafers. I stuck the boning knife in my belt. The water was beginning to boil. I got out a breakfast mug and spooned in instant coffee and sugar and (remembering the dirty cup in Fago's dirty sink) a dollop of milk. I filled the mug with boiling water and stirred. I dropped in the four yellow Elavil tablets and stirred again. I took a tiny sip. It tasted all right, like nothing but instant coffee.

I juggled the shooting jacket bundle and the mug of coffee, and got the key from the nail on the porch. I went down the steps into full morning light and around to the cellar door. The grass was bright with frosty dew. I squatted down, and listened. Nothing. I unlocked the padlock and opened the top door a good crack, and listened. Still nothing. I heaved back both the doors. The steps, the foot of the steps, the lumpy foot of the cot emerged in the fall of light. Fago was still in bed, still asleep. I went quickly down. I dropped the bundle of clothes on the floor and set the coffee on the bottom step. I moved over to the head of the cot.

I said: "Wake up, Ed!"

Fago stirred and grunted. He sat up with a wild start. He saw me standing there. His face began to work. He kicked off the blanket and swung his feet to the floor, and lunged. I saw him coming in plenty of time. I got my foot on his collarbone and shoved. He tumbled back

against the wall. I showed him my knife. He stayed
where he was. But he looked at me like a dog on a
chain.

He said: "You motherfucker—what are you trying to
do to me?"

"I've brought you some coffee, Ed."

"Fuck your coffee."

"And some decent clothes."

"Fuck your clothes, too."

I stood and looked at him.

"And fuck you," he said. "Whoever the fuck you are.
Who are you, anyway?"

I smiled a pleasant smile.

"I asked you a question, motherfucker."

His heart wasn't really in it, though. His face relaxed.
It softened and collapsed. He looked like a man who
had lost his way.

He said: "Jesus Christ—where am I? What *is* this?"

"I told you, Ed. He wants to see you."

"I don't know what you mean," he said. His mouth
gave a sudden twitch. "You got the wrong guy. I don't
know anybody like you're talking about."

"He knows *you*, Ed."

I took a careful step back, and picked up the mug of
coffee.

"Here," I said, and held it out. But I kept my knife
in sight in my other hand. "You'll feel better when
you've had some coffee."

He sat there, hunched back against the gray stone
cellar wall. His face began to change. It tightened with

thought, with resolution. It tightened—and then abruptly loosened. It fell apart. He had lost his way again.

"Come on," I said. "Take your coffee."

He sat and stared. His mouth twitched. He took a deep breath, and put out his hand and took the mug. He took a swallow. He seemed to like it all right. He took another, bigger swallow. He wiped his mouth with the back of his hand, his left hand, and I caught a glimpse of a watch with a silver metal band. That was something to remember.

He said: "What's he want to see me about?"

"I don't know," I said. "He didn't tell me. Now come on—finish your coffee, and get out of those clothes. He wants to see you looking halfway decent."

He looked at his jeans, his T-shirt. "I don't see anything wrong with my clothes."

"I do," I said. "And so would he. You've slept in them. Finish your coffee, Ed."

He took a gulp, and handed over the mug. He tried to glare at me.

"O.K., Ed. Now—the shirt."

He pulled it off, and then his jeans. I gathered them up, and a thick brown wallet fell out on the floor. I kicked it my way, and picked it up. Fago gave a little yell.

"I'll keep it for you," I said.

I moved to the steps.

"Hey—where are you going?"

I backed up the steps.

"I'll be back directly," I said. "Just see that you're dressed and ready."

▲◀

Arlene was up. I could hear her walking in the bedroom overhead. I hoped she wouldn't hurry, I hoped she would take her time. I didn't feel like talking. I put the kettle on to boil again and washed out Fago's mug and fixed myself some coffee. It was something to do until the Elavil began to take hold. But I couldn't drink it. I couldn't get it down. My throat was too thick and tight. After a gagging swallow, I got up and emptied the mug in the sink and washed it again and put it away. I sat down and lighted a cigarette. I sat there and smoked and tried to keep my mind an empty blank, and waited.

And then I couldn't wait any longer. I couldn't just sit and not think. I got rid of my cigarette. I felt along the closet shelf for my gloves, my worn and supple pigskin gloves, and put them on and opened the table drawer and removed the final, pristine version of the note from its newspaper covering and went out and around to the cellar and unlocked and opened the doors. I took a cautious look. Fago, in my yesterday's shirt and trousers and with my old shooting jacket folded on his lap, was sitting on the rumpled end of the cot. His head was dropped on his chest. I went down the steps in a couple of jumps, waving the note in my hand. He lifted his head and opened his mouth, he started to say something, but I didn't give him time.

I said: "God damn it—just take a look at this!"

He said: "What—what's the matter?"

I held out the note, thrust it at him, upside down and wrong side up.

"Plenty," I said. "Just look! Take a good look!"

He said: "What—what is it?"

"Take it!"

He raised a heavy hand and took it. He looked blankly at the blank back side. He turned it over and looked again. He paused and thought and turned it around.

I said: "Oh, for God's sake—I thought you could read!"

He looked blankly up.

"Never mind," I said. "Give it here." I reached out and took a corner of the paper between my thumb and forefinger. "Let go!"

He let go.

He said: "I . . ."

But I was halfway up the steps. I slammed and locked the doors, and carried the fluttering paper carefully back to the house.

▲◢

Arlene opened the door for me. She wore no make-up, and her hair looked almost wild. She had on slacks and a sweater that looked as if she had taken them out at random and put them on in the dark. She looked just right.

"I heard you talking," she said. "I heard your voice. Is everything . . .?"

I only nodded. My mind was too full to look back. I went over and dropped the note face up on the table. I looked around, and picked up the kitchen salt shaker and rubbed it clean with my glove, and put it on the note for a weight.

I turned to Arlene. "O.K."

She picked up the shaker and put it down. She picked up the note in both hands and shifted her hold a fraction and put it down again. She toppled the shaker carefully, wildly, across it.

"Good," I said.

I coughed to clear my throat. My chest was so tight I could hardly breathe, and I had a tense, heavy feeling in my scrotum, like a weight between my legs. I went over to the closet and took out my gun. I found a shell and loaded one of the barrels. I ran my gloved hand up and down the barrels, along the stock, around the hammers and triggers.

"Well," I said.

Arlene stood looking at me, breathing hard.

"Chick," she said. "Oh, Chick!"

It was full light now, but cold, still cold. I opened the cellar doors again and threw them back. But this time I didn't go down.

I called out: "O.K., Ed—come on up."

Fago got heavily off the cot and struggled into my jacket. He mumbled something, like a man talking in his sleep. He came slowly, heavily up the steps. He stopped with a jerk, and focused his eyes in a stare.

"Hey!" he said. He licked his lips and swallowed. "What's that fucking gun for?"

"That's the way he likes it," I said. "He doesn't take any chances." I poked the gun at his belly. But gently, playfully. "Come on—let's get going."

"Don't do that!"

He grabbed the gun and pushed it violently away. I poked it back and let him grab it again. That took care of the barrel.

"All right," I said. "This way, Ed."

We headed back around the house, past the garage, down the back lawn.

I said: "I don't know how much you know about guns . . ."

"Huh?"

"This is quite a gun," I said. I offered it to him, butt first. "Just feel that stock. Go on—feel it!"

He gave it a gingerly touch.

"Come on," I said. "Take a good grip. That's genuine shagbark hickory."

"Yeah?" he said. "Hey—that's all water down there.

That's Accabonac Pond. Where the fuck are we going?"

It was the end of the mowed lawn, the beginning of the meadow and the long slope down to the water, the view that had always been my favorite.

I said: "We're stopping right here."

"I thought . . ."

I brought the gun around. I cocked it and jabbed the muzzle hard in his belly.

"Back up against that tree."

"*Hey . . . !*"

But he backed.

I shifted the gun, straightened it up, got the muzzle of the loaded barrel tight under his chin. Fago was saying something, was trying to say something, but I couldn't hear. There was a sound in my ears like a waterfall. I leaned back and away as far as I could. I got my thumb on the trigger, and squeezed. The waterfall soared, roared to a tidal wave. I didn't have to drop the gun. It fell, slipped, vanished from my hands.

I stood for an instant, trying to breathe. I didn't look; nothing could have made me look. Then I squatted down and felt and found the watch on his wrist and took it off and strapped on mine instead. Then I pulled off my gloves and pushed and worked and twisted and got them on his hands. Then I got up and stood and looked and listened. Silence. Only silence. Sunday-morning silence.

I took a gulping breath, and started back to the house. I told myself that Arlene was right. I told myself that nothing meant anything anymore. There was no more right. There was no more wrong. There were only opportunities. There was only one's own survival. I broke into a kind of run. I told myself I didn't feel a thing.

TWO

1

I stood at the bedroom window with the curtain drawn a scant inch open, and watched the police car coming. They hadn't wasted any time. Arlene had called at most ten minutes ago. I watched the car slow at the mailbox and then turn sharply into the driveway. It pulled up just short of the cellar door. The driver was a man in uniform, a young man with thick dark hair and a heavy mustache, and he was alone. I watched him reach for his radiotelephone. I watched him speak and nod and hang up. I watched him get out and put on his cap, and head for the kitchen door. I watched him out of sight. I was only a watcher, an observer, now. I had done what I had to do, what had to be done, and I was finished. It now was Arlene's turn—now and from now on.

I moved across the bedroom, walking softly in my stocking feet, to the back window. There was nothing to see. The kitchen door was directly below the window. But I could hear—a little. I heard steps on the porch, a commanding knock, the back door creaking open. I heard the rumble of the officer's voice. I heard

Arlene. I heard her say something, a wild rush of words, and then break off. She gave a kind of sob. There was another, shorter rumble, and the officer came into my view, backing away. He turned and hopped briskly down the steps. I watched him striding down the lawn —toward the rise, toward the big bare apple tree, toward the beginning of the meadow. I watched him suddenly stop. I watched him take another step or two, and stop again. Then he swung around. He came back up the lawn, heading for his car, for his radio, almost trotting. His face above the big mustache was the color of cement.

I moved back from the window, and sat down on the bed. I wanted a cigarette. I wanted a drink. I wanted —I didn't know what I wanted. I was tired. I was exhausted. I was too old for this. I wanted to sleep, to go to sleep and sleep for a week. But I couldn't even sit. I had been wound up too long. I got up and took a cautious turn around the room. I went out and into the bathroom. I went back to the bedroom. I heard the sound of another car in the driveway. I heard a car door slam. I moved to the side window. I looked down through the blur of the curtain at another, bigger, older officer, a sergeant. I watched the two of them talking. The younger officer took notes in a notebook. He went back to his car, to his radio, again. The sergeant walked a few steps down the back lawn. He stood as still as a stone for a moment, and then headed for the house. I went back and sat down on the bed. I sat there with my hands hanging limp and loose between my legs. I heard another car arrive. And then another. I heard voices in the kitchen, voices out back, voices on the drive. I made myself stay put on the bed. I couldn't risk the windows now. There were too many watchful eyes, too many listening ears.

▶ ◀

I awoke to a thump, to the sound of the back door slamming. I opened my eyes to twilight. I came fully, awarely, awake. It couldn't be morning; it was late afternoon, early evening. I had slept through most of the day. I lay there wondering. I heard steps on the stairs. The sound of the door slammed again in my mind, and my heart tripped. I rolled off the bed and stood up. The light went on. Arlene came into the room.

"Oh," I said. My heart stumbled back to normal. "I heard the door. I didn't know what . . ."

Arlene said: "It's all right."

She sat limply down on the bed.

"I've been over at the Talmadges'," she said. "They couldn't have been more—wonderful. It was awful."

"The *Talmadges?*"

She nodded. "Chick—it was just awful. They even wanted me to spend the night."

I dropped back on the bed beside her.

"Look," I said. "I don't understand any of this. What were you doing at the Talmadges'?"

"I couldn't help it. They came over and got me. They heard about it from the police—about you. And they knew we were from away, that I was alone. So they were being good neighbors. That's what made it so awful."

"Arlene," I said. "Tell me what happened. What were the police doing at the Talmadges'?"

She looked at me. "They were everywhere," she said. "There must have been a dozen of them. Including the chief—Chief Horne. They took pictures, they took measurements, they got down on their knees and crawled around in the grass. Thank God we didn't take any chances. They even had a special plastic bag for the note, to protect it. And they all talked to me, asked me questions, the same questions, about your state of mind and what happened to your job and had I suspected anything like this and they were very interested to know about Dr. Chandler, and they wrote down every word I said. Then I had to go down there—down to the apple tree. I had to go down there and identify it. I really didn't like that very much."

She raised her shoulders, and let them drop.

I waited.

She said: "Actually, they were terribly polite. They acted almost sympathetic. But I don't know—they're so different from everybody else. Especially the detective. I never dreamed there would be a detective. He was the one that went over and talked to the Talmadges."

"Oh?"

"I don't know what he expected. It turned out they hadn't seen a thing. They were in bed asleep. They didn't even hear the shot. But it's funny—they thought

82

there was something wrong with you."

"Wrong? What do you mean—wrong?"

"They didn't come right out and say it. But I got the impression that there's been some talk about you lately. That you'd been acting funny or different or something. I don't know what exactly—and it doesn't matter. What matters is that they told it to the detective. I think it impressed him."

"Yes," I said.

"Well, anyway," she said. She ran her fingers through her tangled hair. "The worst thing was the waiting. That was really a strain. They only left a couple of hours ago. I finally sat down and covered my face and acted as if I was on the verge of hysterics. They had to wait first for the doctor. Then they had to wait for the medical examiner. Then they had to wait for his van. Which had to come all the way from the county offices at Hauppauge. That was for the body. They call it the morgue wagon."

I didn't say anything. We both were silent for a moment. Then Arlene put her hand on mine. She smiled a serious smile.

"It went all right," she said. "I'm sure of that, Chick. We did it."

"What happens next?"

"They're going to do an autopsy. Tomorrow, I think. But that doesn't mean anything. It's something they always do in a case like this. Then the undertaker takes over."

We sat together on the edge of the bed. It gave me

a peculiar feeling to think that people had been talking about me. It was a piece of luck—wonderful luck. But it gave me a peculiar feeling all the same.

Arlene smiled and squeezed my hand.

She said: "You haven't had anything to eat. I'll go fix you something."

I shook my head. "No," I said. "I'm not hungry."

"Oh?" she said. "Neither am I. But I had something at the Talmadges'."

▶◀

The telephone rang. We sat startled, rigid, on the edge of the bed. It rang wildly out again.

Arlene said: "Oh, God—who do you suppose that is?"

"You'd better answer it," I said. "It might be important."

"All right," she said.

And ran. I followed her out and down the hall to the head of the stairs. The telephone rang again, and cut off.

Arlene said: "Hello? Yes?"

I waited, listening.

Then: "Gloria! Oh, my dear, I didn't recognize your . . ."

A pause.

Then: "Oh, Gloria! Oh, my God!" Her voice broke. "You'll never know!"

A long pause.

Then: "I know, dear—I know. Of course I do. And I

84

knew you would. It's been so awful. These last few weeks have been so—I mean, just watching the poor darling." Her voice broke again. "But—I never dreamed."

A longer pause.

Then: "Oh, Gloria, you're so sweet. Just to hear your voice. But no—really, I'd rather not. Maybe in a week or two or something. No, I mean it, dear. And I'm really not all that alone. I have these simply wonderful neighbors, this young couple next door—George and Rita Talmadge. They've been absolutely wonderful."

A pause.

Then: "Yes, I do—I truly do. I promise. And give my love to Paul. I can't tell you how much . . ."

A pause.

Then: "I know. Yes. Goodbye."

I heard her hang up. She came around to the stairs, and up.

She said: "That was Gloria."

"So I gathered," I said. "But how in the hell . . .?"

Arlene smiled.

"The police called her," she said. "That detective. I gave him their name. I thought we could use another witness."

▲◄

Arlene turned over, squirmed, and put her arms around me. I could feel her soft breasts flattened against my back. I felt a spark. It glowed, flickered, and went out.

"Chick—are you awake?"

I was awake, wide awake, but I only grunted.

"I'm cold," she said. "I'm freezing."

I gave another, sympathetic grunt.

"Chick?"

I knew what she meant. But I said: "Do you want me to close the window?"

"No," she said. "I want you to turn over. I want you to come here."

I felt her warm, searching hand. But I felt nothing, nothing at all. I lay there tense and limp.

"Chickie . . ."

I had to say it. I said: "I—I can't."

There was an instant of screaming silence.

She said: "What do you mean, you can't?"

"I just can't."

She moved. Her hand came away. She hit me hard on the hip with her fist.

"Damn you," she said.

"I'm sorry," I said.

She lay stiffly beside me. I could hear her breathing. Then she moved again. She fitted herself against the line of my back.

"I'm sorry," she said. "I didn't mean it, Chick."

I sat on the sofa and stared at the empty fireplace, at the shiny black patina of soot, and listened to Arlene rummaging in the drawer of the desk behind me. She was looking for my Social Security card. The drawer closed. She went back to the telephone.

She said: "Mr. Temple? Well, I finally found it. His number is six five eight dash one five dash four four three three. That's right—four four three three."

She nodded.

She said: "Yes, I see. Well, yes. We have talked about it, and my husband—we both thought we would prefer cremation. So yes—I guess so."

She looked across at me, and made a frowning face.

She said: "Well—we're rather new here, you know. I mean, we don't really know many people. I mean, I don't really think a regular service would be—you know—expected. Actually, I don't think I could stand it. I mean, in the circumstances. Yes. That's right."

She nodded again, still looking at me, still frowning.

She said: "Oh? Oh, I see. Oh, yes—of course. I mean, I hadn't really thought. What would you—suggest? Oh, you do? Yes. That would be fine. I'll come in sometime tomorrow. Thank *you*. Goodbye."

She hung up, and slumped drained in her chair.

I said: "What's happening tomorrow?"

"I have to pick out an urn," she said. "For your ashes."

My mind began to dull, and drifted off the page again. It was like a kind of uneasy sleep. I got up and went out to the kitchen and got myself a drink of water. Arlene had gone into the village—to the bank, to the store, to the Temple Funeral Home. I stood at the sink with the glass in my hand. It was the first time I had been alone in the house, and I felt exposed and vulnerable.

I went back to my chair and picked up my book. It was a copy of *Treasure Island*. I had found it in a box of Charlie's old books in the attic, and remembered its faraway and undemanding magic. I found my place and drove myself back to the Admiral Benbow Inn. I dodged and waited behind the open door with Black Dog. I saw the Black Spot thrust into the Captain's trembling hand. I saw the five riders come over the rise in the moonlight, and I heard blind Pew's dying scream. I felt the magic taking solid hold. I half heard the sound of an approaching car. I heard it slow. I heard it come to a stop out front.

Black Hill Cove was gone in an instant, and instantly forgotten. I sank low in my chair, low enough to be out of sight from any window. But I wondered who would park on the road. It could hardly be anyone we knew. Even the police had parked on the driveway. I glanced toward the dining room, in the direction of the kitchen, waiting for the knock on the kitchen door. I waited— and heard steps on the front door stoop. This couldn't be anyone we knew. There was a good knock on the door. There was a pause, and then another, harder knock. There was another pause, a longer pause, and a final, half-hearted knock. The footsteps crossed the stoop again. I slid out of my chair and ducked across and knelt at the front window.

I looked out at a man in a belted trenchcoat and a little tweed hat on his head. I watched his wide back going down the path. I wondered if he could be Arlene's detective. But would a detective have come like this—in an ordinary car, to the front door, unannounced? I thought he probably would.

The man reached his car. He hesitated, and looked back toward the house. And I knew him. He was Alva J. Bennett of the Bennett Agency. He was the real estate broker from whom we had bought our house almost two years ago.

I watched him go on and around the car and get in and drive slowly off. I stood up and stretched. I realized I was smiling. Mr. Bennett had given me a little scare, but I easily forgave him for that. He had also given me an encouraging piece of news. It apparently was accepted behavior for a recent widow to promptly sell her house.

▲ ◢

The little mail delivery van scooted off down the road, and Arlene came back up the path. She was walking slowly with a couple of letters stuck under her arm and the East Hampton *Star* folded open. She came to a stop, and stood there reading. She closed the paper and came on and up the steps and in. She dropped the mail on the table and handed me the *Star*.

"It's on the second page," she said.

I opened the paper and found the page. I felt Arlene watching me. It was the first story in the obituary column. It was headed "Charles L. Hill," and it read:

Charles Landon Hill, a retired New York advertising executive, was found dead in a meadow behind his home on Fireplace Road, Springs, at 8:30 A.M. Sunday. A shotgun from which one shot had been fired lay at his side. Police said a note addressed to his wife indicated that he had taken his own life. He was 62.

Mr. Hill and his wife, the former Arlene Crawford, moved here from New York about two years ago. At the time of his retirement, Mr. Hill was a senior research executive in the firm of Lambert Tucker Associates. He was the author of a novel, *Bring On Your Harvest*, published in 1949. He was born in Fulton, Mo., and was graduated from Kemper Military School and the University of Missouri. In World War II, he served in the Army in the Middle East and elsewhere, and was discharged with the rank of Captain.

A son, Lieut. Charles L. Hill, Jr., USAF, was reported missing in action in Vietnam in 1970.

I read my obituary through again. It was strange. I had expected a certain impact, a sense of voyeuristic shock. I felt a pang, as always, at the sight of Charlie's name. But that was all. I might have been rereading the biographical note on the foxed and faded dust jacket of *Bring On Your Harvest.* I put the paper down. Arlene was still watching me. I cleared my throat and tried to smile.

I said: "I wouldn't say he'd had much of a life, would you?"

Arlene gave a little shrug.

"Maybe he can do better next time," she said.

2

Arlene hung up the telephone, and came smiling back to the sofa.

"That was Fred Fitch," she said. "About your insurance."

"Oh?"

She sat down and picked up her glass. "He said he'd been trying to get me all afternoon."

"Could be," I said. "The phone did ring a couple of times."

"Well," she said. "Anyway—everything seems to be O.K. He was only waiting for a copy of the death certificate. He's sending the stuff all off to the company tomorrow. They make the payment from Hartford." She took a quick sip of her drink. "He asked me how I wanted it. I said I thought the lump sum. And all he said was O.K."

"It's a pretty good lump," I said.

"Yes." But she said it in a funny way.

I said: "You don't think so?"

"Yes," she said. "Of course I do. The only thing is—

Mr. Fitch said there was a certain amount of processing involved. He said it might take up to three weeks."

"Three weeks!"

"That's what he said."

"Good God," I said. "I can't live holed up like this for three more weeks."

"I don't think you should."

"What do you mean?"

"I mean—well, I never really thought it was such a good idea for us to leave here together."

"Oh?"

"I don't think we ever really thought about it," she said. "We just sort of took it for granted. I know I did."

"Well?"

"I'm beginning to think it might be risky—awfully risky."

"Mmmm . . ."

"Besides," she said, "it would give you a chance to sort of look around and find a place—the right kind of place. That's going to take a little time, you know."

I thought for a moment.

"All right," I said. "I think you have a point. I think you're probably right. But how am I going to get out of here? You want me to take the bus? You want me to take the train?"

"No," she said. "I don't mean that. I mean . . ."

She sat with her drink in her hand. She took an absent-minded swallow. She gave a kind of purr. She looked up.

She said: "What about Fago's car?"

I looked at her.

"It's just sitting there," she said. "And you've got the keys."

I nodded.

"As a matter of fact," she said. "I think it might be better if it weren't just sitting there."

I nodded.

"Well?" she said. She looked at me across her glass. "Well, what do you think?"

"I don't know," I said. "I just wonder if . . ."

I stopped. I didn't wonder anything. I knew.

I put down my drink and stood up.

"What did I do with Fago's wallet?" I said. "Where did we put it?"

"What?"

"Fago's wallet—where is it?"

"It's in the kitchen," she said. "It's in the dish towel drawer—with the money. Why?"

"I'll be right back."

I went out to the kitchen and fumbled through the dish towels and under the money envelope, and it was there. I folded it open to a little crumple of currency and dug into the pockets. There were four of them and they were jammed full—clippings, receipts, scribbled addresses, scribbled telephone numbers, scribbled memorandums, a condom, a plastic calendar for 1973, an overexposed snapshot of a girl in a pageboy hairdo. But I found what I was looking for.

I went back to the living room. Arlene watched me coming. She sat expectantly erect, smiling a bright,

94

puzzled, expectant smile. I sat down beside her at the coffee table. I dealt out the first of the two cards—Fago's Social Security card. I waited half a second. Then I trumped it with his driver's license.

Arlene looked down at the cards. She picked up the driver's license, and put it carefully down again. She looked at me. "This is perfect, Chick," she said. "This is absolutely perfect."

"Well," I said.

I needed one more card to be complete. I needed the car registration. But that would be in the car, in the glove compartment. And I had the key to that, too.

I reached out and knocked on the wood of the table.

"We'll see," I said.

▶ ◀

I emptied Fago's suitcase out on the guest room floor and carried it into the bedroom and spread it open on the bed. I didn't relish using it, but it was capacious enough and sturdy enough, and it didn't, like mine, have a telltale set of initials. Arlene had laid out my clothes—three pairs of chinos, my seersucker jacket, my summer suit. I added some short-sleeved shirts and jerseys, and a pair of swimming trunks. I might have been packing for a winter vacation. Except, of course, I wasn't. It was winter, or almost winter, and I was going south, to Florida. But the difference was, I wouldn't be coming back.

I walked over to the window. I wasn't sorry to go. I

was ready, more than ready. And this was a good day for going. I looked out at the fading afternoon—at the quilted gray sky and the bare-boned trees, at the yellowing lawn and the browning meadow, at the cold steel glint of the pond. There was nothing here that I would ever miss.

I heard Arlene calling me.

I let the curtain drop. I got my hound's-tooth jacket out of the closet. I closed the suitcase and locked it and picked up my old attaché case. I looked around the bedroom for the last time, and went out and down to the kitchen.

Arlene was closing the refrigerator door. She had a tray of ice cubes in her hand. There were bottles and glasses on the table.

"It's still too light to leave," she said. "I thought we could have a little goodbye drink."

"All right," I said.

I sat down at the table and watched her fix the drinks. She came over with my drink. I put my arm around her waist and held her for a moment.

"I wish I weren't going alone."

"I know," she said.

"I really do."

"I know, Chick."

"It's going to be a long three weeks."

"Yes," she said. She sat down with her drink. "You've got your money?"

I nodded. "It's in my little bag." I took a swallow of

my drink. "I hate taking the whole thing."

"I'll be all right," she said. "I can always get an advance or something." She smiled at me across the table. "As a matter of fact, I already have."

"Oh?"

"I went in to see Fred Fitch this morning. He's a real friend."

She put down her glass. She reached in the pocket of her sweater and handed me an envelope with the springy feel of money. I lifted the flap and looked in. The bills were fifties. There seemed to be eight or ten of them.

I said: "Arlene! For heaven's sake . . ."

"I didn't dare ask for more."

"I don't need this," I said. "I've already got more than enough."

"I want you to be comfortable," she said.

I went out first with my bags. Arlene had left the car in the driveway to block the view from the Talmadge house. I stayed in the lee of the car and kept my head well down. I shoved the bags in back, and ducked into the passenger's seat in front. I turned up my raincoat collar and slid down as low as I could. I could see the lights of the Talmadge house through the web and grille of the hedgerow, but they were only a curtained glow. I heard Arlene coming. She opened the door and got quickly in. She gave my thigh a couple of pats, and started the engine. We backed slowly out of the driveway.

I stayed hunched down in my seat. There was always traffic at this time of day on Fireplace Road. I sat and gazed up through the windshield at the early-evening stars. The sky was high and black and the stars were very bright. It was going to be a cold night. And a long one. I had to be across the Verrazano Bridge and well down on the Jersey Turnpike before I could safely stop. But first I had to get safely out of town. I hoped there was gas in Fago's car—enough to get me started on my way. I remembered the feel of the wheel, the heaviness, the drag of what might be a broken spring. I hoped the car would last the trip. But I couldn't really worry. What I really felt was a quickening, a zest, an excitement. I was up and out and moving. I had something to do. I had a future again.

The traffic thinned and the scrubby woods closed in. We made the turn into Cedar Pond Road. There was nobody behind us, nobody ahead. I sat up and stretched. Beyond the thrust of the headlights, the enclosing trees had an impenetrable, jungle look. I felt a twist of tension. This was the really risky part. The view opened up ahead. The meadow emerged from the dark. Arlene slowed.

I said: "Maybe you ought to cut your lights."
"O.K."

The road went black, but the meadow showed the way. The house loomed, and then the car in the driveway. Arlene pulled in behind it and stopped, but left the engine running. I got out. The only sound was the idling engine and I stood surrounded by night. I got my bags and carried them over and loaded them into Fago's car. I went back to Arlene. She rolled down the window and pulled down my head and gave me a lingering kiss.

She sat abruptly back.

She said: "You've got to go."

"Arlene," I said. "I . . ."

"I know," she said. "I know."

"Goodbye."

"Goodbye," she said. "And take care—Ed."

3

It began to rain as I came off the Verrazano Bridge, and it rained all the long way down the Jersey Turnpike. Around one o'clock, I gave up. I spent the rest of the night in a truckers' motel, an island of wild green mercury glare, on the outskirts of Wilmington. It was cold in my room, and there were voices and footsteps and slammed doors and backfires and the cry of air brakes all night long. I got up twice and looked out the window to make sure that my car was still there. I left the next morning in the same green blaze of light. But the rain had stopped. And by the time I got through Baltimore, the sun was up and out, and I felt released again.

I spent the second night in North Carolina, in Fayetteville, at a Holiday Inn. I had country ham with red-eye gravy for dinner, and in the morning, for the first time in twenty years, I had grits for breakfast. That kept me going all day. I stayed that night somewhere south of Brunswick, Georgia, and early the next afternoon, I had my first sight of the Gulf. I took off my jacket and rolled up my shirt sleeves. I drove under palms and live oaks and the rise of condominiums. I drove along a head-high hedge spangled with starry white flowers. Framed midway in the hedge, like a state historical marker, was a blue-and-white sign: "Warning! Oleander Plants Are Poisonous. Do Not Cut or Burn." I drove through Crystal River and New Port Richey and Tarpon Springs. I came into Dunedin. I got a closer and a bluer look at the Gulf. A man in work clothes, real work clothes, gave me a civil look. A sign the size of a No Parking sign read: "This Community Is a Bird Sanctuary." I had the feeling I had come to the right place. It was, at any rate, a place to start. I turned off the highway, away from the water, away from the beachfront opulence. I drove down a densely verdant residential street. I crossed a deserted intersection. There was a planting just ahead of blazing hibiscus bushes almost the size of trees. There was a kind of totem pole with a pagoda sign on top: "Hibiscus Gardens Motel." There was a steakhouse restaurant across the street, and a liquor store on the corner. I turned into Hibiscus Gardens.

I had dinner that night at the steakhouse restaurant. I had a drink at the bar and then another at the table, and ordered the special steak. I knew I was back in the South. The steak was the thickness of a slice of bread and it was the texture almost of Melba toast. After dinner, I took a walk. It was hard to remember where I was, and why. There was a summery smell of flowers in the mild evening air, and the sound from hidden houses of television talk and gunshots and laughter. I circled back to the motel. I found my room and went in and sat down on the one big chair. I sat and looked at the telephone on the bedside table. All I had to do was pick it up, and in a minute or two I would hear her voice. It would have been enough just to hear her voice. But it wouldn't be wise. It wouldn't be safe. We had agreed on that.

I got undressed and got into bed. It was a king-size double bed with a Magic Fingers vibrator attachment. I got back up and found a quarter and put it in the slot. The bed began to gently heave. I thought of Arlene again. It brought a clutch of longing to my throat. It was a ridiculous feeling for a man of my age, but that was the way I felt.

▲ ◢

The clerk on morning duty at the Hibiscus Gardens was a tall young woman with long pale hair and a tight mouth. Her name, according to a wooden sign on the desk, was Miss Rockne. She gave me a suspicious look.

"Good morning," I said. "Can you tell me where I can get some breakfast?"

"Breakfast?" she said. Her look changed from suspicion to pity. "I'm sorry, but we don't serve food here."

I took a patient breath. "I know," I said. "But . . ."

The telephone rang. Miss Rockne stiffened and swooped and caught it on the echo.

"Good morning," she said. "Hibiscus Gardens."

Her face flushed, her eyes brightened, her mouth softened.

She said: "Oh! Oh—just a minute."

She turned to me with a radiant look.

"There's a terrific place called Henty's," she said. "It's over on Main Street. That's only a couple of blocks. Turn right at the corner and go straight. You can't miss it."

She gave me an engulfing smile. She took up the telephone again, and turned her back.

Henty's was part of a block-long shopping center. The orange juice was frozen and the coffee was weak. But the waitress brought me what I ordered and just the way I ordered it, and the center itself was conveniently comprehensive for my needs. It included two real estate offices, one at each end, a barbershop, a coin laundry, and a standard American bookstore: paperbacks, stationery, greeting cards, gifts. I bought a package of paper and envelopes there, and the cashier told me how to find the post office. I was glad of her help. The post office was a long, low building, mostly glass, and it could easily have been mistaken for an automobile showroom. I parked in what might have been the used car lot, and went in and bought stamps and found a secluded corner counter. It wasn't going to be an easy letter to write. There was nothing, and everything, to say. I addressed the envelope first. I wrote in a round, girlish backhand—what my mother used to call a boarding school hand. I thought it looked exactly the way I wanted it to. Then I stood and looked at the blank square of writing paper. I decided not to say too much. I decided to make it a simple report. I decided to make it something in between. I wrote:

Dear Arlene:

I got here late yesterday afternoon. My trip, thank God, was uneventful. This is a very pleasant little town on the Gulf Coast near Tampa called Dunedin. Everything is Scottish, especially the streets—Aberdeen, Douglas, Highland, Inverness, St. Andrews. It may be just the place for us. I'm staying at the Hibiscus Gardens Motel—inexpensive and O.K. I'm going to start in on the agents this afternoon. Write me care of General Delivery, and write soon. The zip code is 33528. I want to know what's happening. Is everything all right? I'm sure it is, but I want to know. When will you be able to leave? Make it soon. It's beautiful here, but lonely. I love and miss you more than I can say.

I started to sign my name, and stopped. I had a sudden thought. I remembered her voice, her smiling goodbye. I could almost hear and see her. I smiled another answering smile, and signed myself: "Ed."

▲◄

I sat on a bench in the occasional shade of a big palmetto, eating the seafood sandwich I had picked up at a drive-in on the way back to Hibiscus Gardens, and watched the bathers in and around the pool. They seemed to be all ages under six and over forty. I wanted to join them—I had never been swimming in November—but not today. House-hunting came first. I was a fully domesticated man; I was programmed for domesticity.

I dumped the remains of my sandwich in a trashcan, and walked back to my room to get my seersucker jacket. The room was dark and cold after the blaze of noon at the pool, and I had to find my jacket almost by feel. My face in the bureau mirror looked ectoplasmic. I squatted down at the bureau and checked the carpet I had loosened underneath to make sure that my money was still there. Crime, according to a chamber of commerce "Visitor's Guide," was practically unheard of in Dunedin, but I checked my money just the same. I got up and went out and locked the door.

A voice, a woman's voice, said: "Well! So *you're* our New Yorker."

I almost jumped, but I held myself tight. I arranged my face, and turned. There was nothing to worry about. She was a smiling, wide-hipped woman in a wet bathing suit and with a wet bathing cap in her hand. Her hair was a striking shade of lavender and her nose was pink and peeling. I seemed to remember seeing her among the sojourners at the pool. She looked to be in her comfortably early fifties. I tried to match her smile.

"What did you say?"

"Don't look so alarmed," she said. "Are you afraid of aggressive women?"

I smiled a little easier.

"You said something about New York."

"I was only matching you and your car," she said. "Which makes you the New Yorker in our little group."

That was agreeable news.

I said: "I'm the only one?"

"You are," she said. "At the moment, anyway. But I hope you won't let it go to your head."

"I think I can take it in stride."

"So—where are you from in New York?"

I hesitated, but only for an instant.

"Long Island," I said.

"Long Island!" she said. "I'm impressed. That's the chic part, isn't it?"

"It's a big island."

"I wouldn't know about that," she said. "I'm from Omaha—Omaha, Nebraska."

"I know about Omaha."

"Do you?" she said. "That's very nice. So many of you Easterners don't."

I shrugged.

"Well," I said. She was an attractive woman, a nice woman, but I had to find a place to live. "I think I'd better . . ."

"Oh, I know," she said. "I can tell by your jacket—you have an appointment."

"That's right," I said. "As a matter of fact, I do."

I smiled and started to move away, across the little covered porch, out and on to my car.

"I'll see you," I said.

She returned my smile, and more. Much more.

"Of course," she said.

▲▲

Mr. Beauchamp (pronounced "Beecham") of Beauchamp & Beauchamp, Realtors, Since 1923, leaned back in his big leather chair and ran his long tanned fingers through his long and faintly graying hair.

"Well, Mr. Fago," he said. "Have I got that right—Fago? An interesting name—sounds French. How do you spell it—no, let me guess. I'll say *F-a-g-e-a-u.*" He gave me a shrewd look. "Or would it be *F-a-g-e-a-u-x?*"

"I'm afraid not," I said. "It's just plain *F-a-g-o.*"

"I see," he said. "It must have got Anglicized somewhere along the line. I don't know how we ever kept ours pure. Just lucky, I guess." He laughed a bark of a laugh. He gave his hair a final rumple, and steepled his hands beneath his chin. "Now then. I understand you're not interested in land. You want something already built. Real fine. So you tell me what you've got in mind and I'll tell you what I've got on hand. We may not be the biggest firm in town, but we're just about the oldest. My daddy founded this business way back yon-

107

der when Dunedin was just a little bitty place, and we've sort of grown up with it. So if anybody knows the market here, I think it most likely is us."

"Good," I said. "What I . . ."

Mr. Beauchamp held up a hand. "However," he said, "I need a little bit of help. Now if I understand you correctly, we're not talking about a rental. Which is just as well. Because there are very few homes for rent here. We've got apartments, of course, but no homes, no houses—practically none. So what we're talking about is a home or a condominium to buy. Now—there are two things I need to know. One is money. How much are you prepared to spend? And the other is this: What are your requirements? But let's take the last one first. How big is your family?"

"I don't exactly have a family," I said. "There are just two of us." I hesitated. It was a little uncomfortable, a little embarrassing for a man of my age, a man of my generation. But it had to be said. "I have a—friend. She'll be joining me in a couple of weeks."

"Fine," he said. "Real fine. And I'm real glad you said 'she.' " He laughed his barking laugh. "We're not quite as liberated down here as you folks are up North. But we're making progress. We've made some headway. I mean, folks in your situation—we're familiar with that. We understand it and we accept it. It's a matter of simple economics. It's a fact of life."

I pricked up my ears. This was interesting.
"Oh?"

"Yes, sir," he said. "We've got a whole lot of retired

108

folks here in Dunedin, a lot of them widows living on their husbands' Social Security and such, so we see it all the time. I had a couple in here a little while back, they must have been up in their seventies. Good, decent, churchgoing folks. And they didn't even bat an eye when they gave me their different names. Well, I say, why the heck should they? We don't make our morals anymore. We can't. They're all made for us up there in Washington by those politicians and bureaucrats—by those tax people and those Social Security people and all the rest. It's enough to make a cat laugh."

I looked at Mr. Beauchamp. It was a look of gratitude. I hadn't known. I hadn't realized. Arlene and I would be nothing out of the ordinary here. We wouldn't have to explain ourselves. There was nothing that needed explaining.

"I think you're right," I said. "You're absolutely right."

"Well," he said. "It's a mess, all right." He smiled a muted smile. He adjusted a paper on his desk. "Now suppose you give me some idea of how much you want to spend."

▲◄

I bought a copy of the Tampa *Tribune* from a vending machine out front, and followed the other midmorning dawdlers into the post office. I glanced at the *Tribune* headlines and read the sunny-and-pleasant weather report, and waited my turn at the General Delivery window. The clerk handed what looked like a bank statement to a portly man in a blue yachting cap, and looked at me.

"Fago," I said. "Edwin Fago. Anything for me?"

The clerk picked up a sheaf of mail as thick as a fist, and shuffled briskly through. He shook his head.

"Nothing," he said. "Sorry."

I thanked him and turned away. I wasn't really disappointed. This was only Wednesday, and I hadn't really expected a letter this soon. She would have had to get my letter on Monday and sit right down and write and mail it off that same day. It had been only a wish, a hope. But tomorrow was possible. It was even almost probable.

I left my car in a parking lot walled around with what I had learned were Australian pines, and went down through a shady sea grape grove and out on a dazzle of white beach. Compared to the miles of beach at Amagansett, it wasn't much of a beach, but I had never seen sand so white, or water so limpidly blue, or felt such limpid ocean air. There were big family groups strung out the length of the beach on the left. I walked down through sand as soft, as feathery as flour, to the edge of the water, and turned to the right.

There was nobody in sight in that direction but one little group of kids. There were three of them—two youths in cut-off blue-jean swimming trunks and a girl. They were lying together on an army blanket, and there were towels spread out and brown paper bags and empty Coke bottles and shirts and sneakers and a cowboy hat and a pile of Sunday papers. As I came toward them, they rolled over and stretched and got up. One of the boys had a piratical black mustache. The girl had the usual thick legs and the usual long, straight hair and the usual sleepwalker stare. She fastened her bikini bra and put on the usual pictorial T-shirt. The boy with the mustache shook out the blanket and folded it up, and the other boy went around and gathered up the towels. I walked past, and turned and looked back. The three of them were standing there. The girl had the cowboy hat on her head. One of the boys reached down and picked up a package of cigarettes. Then they started up the beach, leaving their litter—the Coke bottles and the paper bags and the scattered Sunday papers—behind. I looked at the mess, and went on. I wasn't exactly shocked. I was mostly just surprised. I might have been back on the beach at Amagansett on a Sunday afternoon in August. I had somehow thought it might be different here.

I spread out my towel and took off my shirt and shoes, and sat down with my back to the litter. I put the slob kids out of my mind. They had, at any rate, left me the beach to myself. I sat for a time looking out at the glorious water, at a sailboat creeping along the horizon, at a pelican perched on a piling. I lay back and closed my eyes and felt the glorious sun warm on my wintery skin. I tried to let my mind go slack; I tried to think of nothing.

I tried, but I couldn't. The condominiums I had seen, and the houses, the down payments and the mortgage arrangements and the maintenance charges, the city tax and the county tax and the homestead tax exemption, all the complexities, all the legalities, stirred and restirred in my mind. And nothing yet was settled. I sat up and lighted a cigarette. I had another appointment with Mr. Beauchamp in the morning. I had to come to some decision. But I wasn't used to such decisions. There had always before been Arlene. The three New York apartments, the summer cottages at Pound Ridge and Fire Island, the house in East Hampton—we had made all those decisions together. I sat in the Florida sun and thought of Arlene in the fog and sleet, in the dark Long Island winter.

But why didn't she write? I wanted to know what was happening. I wanted to know when to expect her. I needed to know her plans. This wasn't like her at all. She was too practical, too efficient, too supremely careful a planner, to procrastinate, to let things drift. I couldn't understand it. It simply wasn't Arlene. I stared at the pelican still patiently perched on its piling. And then it dawned on me. Of course it wasn't Arlene. It couldn't be Arlene. It was the hopeless United States Postal Service. They had done again the one thing they seemed to do well. They had managed to lose my letter.

I looked at my watch—at Fago's watch. It was ten

minutes after three. I got into my clothes and gathered up my towel. I felt sick. I could see her running out to the mailbox. I could see her walking back. I could see her wondering, worrying, trying to understand. But if I could get a letter into the mail this afternoon, she would certainly have it by Tuesday.

▲◀

We turned off Kirkcaldy Drive into Rob Roy Circle, and pulled up in front of a cavelike opening in a jungle of flowering hedge. Beyond the hedge rose the naked trunks and ferny tops of palms. The house, like all but the biggest houses in Dunedin, was invisible. Mr. Beauchamp waved me through the gateway.

"When I was a boy," he said, "heck, when I was in *high* school, all this land around here was just plowed ground. So you can see how this little old town of ours has grown. And this house here is a brand-new listing. I've hardly even seen it myself."

We crossed a lawn of scrubby grass. There was the sound of birds in the hedge and high overhead the palm leaves creaked and crackled. Mr. Beauchamp brought out his string of keys and opened a faded pink door in a wall of flowering shrubs. We stepped into an empty room with a row of French windows along the far wall.

"Well," Mr. Beauchamp said, "this room, of course, is the living room. The living *and* dining room, I should say. The kitchen is through that doorway on the left. And that open serving counter there is a real convenient touch. The two bedrooms and the bath are . . ."

I could hear him, but I was no longer listening. I was looking across the room, I was looking at the wall of French windows. The windows gave on a garden—a shady walled garden that ran the width of the house. I left Mr. Beauchamp and walked over to the windows. The garden was paved with rosy old brick. There was a little fountain in the center, and it was planted with flowering shrubs and vines and what looked like a lemon tree. I stood there looking, staring, drinking it in. It looked European, Mediterranean. It looked like Renoir and Monet and all the other Impressionists Arlene loved so much. It was a garden made for her—for us. I hardly needed to see any more of the house to know that I'd found our place.

▲ ◢

I woke up with the dream on the tip of my mind. It stayed with me through shaving, through showering, through dressing. I could still feel the shock of the empty cache, the bottom dropping out of my stomach. It was too vivid a dream, too real, too possible, to dismiss. It clung like a premonition.

It was a little too early in the morning for the maids to be on their rounds. But I went to the door and looked out anyway. There was nobody in sight but a gardener. I went back in the room and knelt down and found the loosened carpet under the bureau, and took out the still-thick envelope. The only question was: how much?

I knew, I had heard, that banks were wary of large deposits in cash. I squatted there like a miser with my hoard in my hand, and considered. It seemed prudent at this point in our new life to attract as little attention as possible. Three hundred dollars? Four hundred? But I knew I would never be comfortable now until I had it all in real safekeeping, and this was after all a time of inflation. I decided to risk another hundred. The bank where I planned to open my account was a mammoth mausoleum of a building just down the street from Henty's, and it had an encouragingly impersonal look. I counted out five hundred dollars. I put the envelope back in its hidey-hole, and stood up. I felt better, easier, already. Next week, next Tuesday, I would deposit another five hundred. It would be good to be able to write a check again. There was something a little shady about a man who could pay only in cash. It made me feel not only secure but respectable.

▲ ◀

There was for once no line at the General Delivery window. The usual clerk stood idle and idly watched me coming across the room. I went up to the counter and stopped and smiled.

"Yes?"

"Oh," I said. I had thought he would know me by now. "Fago—Edwin Fago. Anything for me?"

He turned. He took up a clutch of letters and riffled quickly through. He put the clutch back in its slot.

115

"Sorry," he said. "Nothing for Fago."

"Thank you," I said.

I walked back across the room, and out. That would seem to be pretty conclusive proof. There could be no question about it now. Arlene had never received my original letter. I was glad that I'd had the good sense to write her again on Sunday.

▲◀

I dropped the keys to the house on Rob Roy Circle off at Beauchamp & Beauchamp, and drove home in a little flurry of late-afternoon traffic—home to Hibiscus Gardens. I had eaten a sandwich lunch in the pink brick garden and dozed away the afternoon in an old deck chair I had found abandoned in one of the bedrooms. This was the second time I had been there since Monday, and I liked it better every time I saw it—the house, and not just the garden, although the garden, of course, made the difference. I was ready almost to accept the kilted and bagpiped name of the street.

I parked in front of my room, and got out. I could hear joyous sounds and voices from the pool. I felt like a swim myself. I needed some way to work up an appetite for another steakhouse dinner.

I heard the sound of footsteps somewhere off behind me.

"Chick!"

It was a man's voice.

It rose an octave. *"Chick!"*

For an instant, it didn't register, didn't penetrate. Then it hit me. I stopped breathing. I felt knee-deep in sand, like a runner in a dream. I made myself turn.

He was a little potbellied man in Madras shorts. He gave me a glance, and took a couple of quick steps down the driveway.

"Chick!" he said with affection. "You devil—where have you been?"

I stood there staring. I stood frozen, melting, sweating. I felt grabbed and held and slowly pulled back from the crumbling edge of the cliff.

The little man gave me another glance. He shook his head and laughed.

"Don't worry," he said. "He won't bite. He's big—but he's just a big old baby."

▲ ◀

"Yes?"

"Fago," I said. "Edwin Fago. Anything for me?"

"How do you spell that?"

He was, I realized, a different clerk.

"F-a-g-o," I said.

He turned away, and I fixed my eyes on a Marine Corps recruitment poster. I didn't want to watch. I wanted to let it happen.

The clerk said: "Nothing for Edwin Fago. Sorry."

I turned and stared at him. It was hard to believe. This was Saturday. She would have had my letter by Tuesday; by Wednesday at the latest.

"Are you sure?" I said. "Would you mind taking another look?"

The clerk shrugged. I supposed he was used to anxieties. He picked up the pack of letters again and wet his thumb. He went slowly through the pack. This time I watched him. But it was no use. He came to the end. He raised his eyes and shook his head.

"Sorry," he said. "Nothing."

I walked faster, trotted, and then the rain began to really come down, and I broke into a run. I made it under the awning of the steakhouse restaurant just in time. It was not only raining, but cold—cool, anyway. And blowing. I had to tug at the door to open it. I could almost believe that it really was December. I hung up my raincoat and sat down in my usual booth and looked around the familiar room at the mostly unfamiliar faces, and told myself that there would surely be a letter on Monday. There had to be. But how was I going to get through tonight and tomorrow and tomorrow night? I tried to think what could have happened. There was probably some very simple explanation. That was always the way. There were any number of possible explanations, all of them simple—all of them, in hindsight, obvious. I lighted a cigarette, and tried to think of one.

A waitress came up and handed me a menu.

"Would you care for a cocktail?"

I ordered a bourbon, and thought again, and called her back.

"Make that a martini instead."

I sat with my drink. When I finished this, I would have another. And after that, another. I could see the rain blowing and battering at the big front window. The front door opened and a woman came in. It was the woman from Omaha. She had a pale-blue raincoat over her lavender head and a big handbag clutched under her arm. She was alone.

She lowered her raincoat, and saw me. She touched her hair. She came smiling down the row of booths.

She said: "Well—hello there."

"Hello."

She seemed to hesitate. She was a cheerful, attractive woman. And I had had too many meals alone. I put down my glass.

"Well," I said. "It looks like we're both alone. Maybe you'd like to join me?"

"I'd love it," she said. "I'd much rather talk than read."

She hung her dripping raincoat on top of mine. She slipped into the opposite seat and arranged her handbag and a paperback book beside her on the table. She looked at my drink.

"Is that a martini?" she said. "Good. I'll have one, too. But I don't even know your name. I'm Martha Rice. My friends all call me Marty."

"My name is Fago," I said. I no longer had to stop and

think about it. It was no longer any effort. I was getting almost used to it. But it still sounded a little strange. "Edwin Fago."

"Edwin?" she said.

"Ed," I said.

"Good," she said. "Much better."

The waitress came with her drink. I handed over my glass for another. Marty took a little sip of her martini.

"This is nice," she said. "I spend so much time alone. I'm a widow—like practically all the other females down here. My husband died three years ago. Now—you've been married. You have that look. But not entirely. So I don't think you're married now. Am I right?"

"Yes," I said. "That's right. I . . ." But that was enough. I didn't want to go any further into that. I reached across the table and picked up her book. There was a picture of a half-naked girl on the cover. The author had a Swedish name. It was a novel. I said: "Is this any good?"

"Do you like murder mysteries?"

I looked again at the book in my hand. I should have known better. The girl on the cover wasn't just naked —she was also screaming. I put it back on the table.

"Not particularly," I said. "I'm really not much of a reader."

"I love them," she said. "I read them all the time. And—I don't know—I seem to like all kinds. I mean, Agatha Christie—I love Agatha Christie and Dorothy Sayers and all those nice English ladies. And I'm crazy about Ross Macdonald. But I like the other kind, too.

120

What I call the psychological kind—the ones that take you into the mind of the murderer. I think they're simply fascinating. But I wonder just how true they are. I mean, who knows what a murderer really thinks?"

I shrugged. "It's hard to say," I said. "I guess it all . . . depends." I lighted a cigarette and shook out the match and dropped it carefully into the ashtray. "My son was murdered."

She gave a gasp. "Oh!" She stared at me across the table. "Oh—how *awful!* Oh, I'm so sorry!"

"That's all right," I said. "How's your drink?"

▶◀

The clerk looked up from the last of the letters.

"Sorry, Mr. Fago," he said. "Nothing today."

I stood there.

"Nothing?"

"No, sir."

I stood there.

A voice behind me said: "Excuse me . . ."

I still stood there.

The clerk said: "If you don't mind, sir. There are other people waiting. . . ."

▶◀

I picked up the telephone, and put it down again. I didn't know what to do. I didn't know what to think. I had never felt so trapped and hobbled. The only certainty was that something was wrong. Something had gone seriously wrong. And I knew that I had somehow known it, sensed it, suspected it all along. The post office this morning had no more than finally confirmed it. Arlene was in some kind of trouble. That was the only conceivable explanation. She couldn't, or dared not, write. But why? I stubbed out my cigarette. That was beside the point. That wasn't the real, the immediate, question. The immediate question was: What should I do?

I lighted another cigarette. It tasted as vile as, or viler than, the last, but I lighted it anyway. I got up and walked over to the window. The gardener was chopping weeds along the hibiscus row. A shriveled old man with a face like the original John D. Rockefeller rolled slowly across the driveway in a wheelchair pushed by an elderly black man in a St. Louis Cardinals baseball cap. A yellow warbler moved like a spark through the shiny depths of a bayberry tree. I thought of the pink brick garden. It seemed already a scene from another life. I was afraid to call, but I had to call. I had to know. I couldn't just sit and wait. I had had enough of that. I made up my mind. I simply had to know.

I went back and sat down on the bed, and picked up the telephone. I dialed the motel office.

"Hibiscus Gardens." It was a woman's voice, a voice with a lilt, a voice I didn't know. "Can I help you?"

"This is Mr. Fago," I said. "I'm in room seventeen. I want to make a long-distance call."

"Surely," she said. "And the number?"

I gave her the number. I cleared my throat—it was tight and dry—and waited. I listened to the astral hums and squeals. I could feel the thump of my heart. I reached for my cigarettes.

"Hello?"

"Arlene?"

"Yes?"

"Arlene—this is Chick."

"*Who?*"

"Chick. This is Chick, Arlene. I had to call. I want to know what's happened. Is something . . .?"

Her voice hardened. "Who is this? Is this some kind of sick joke? I don't know anybody named Chick—except my husband. And my husband is dead."

"Arlene, listen. . . ."

But she had hung up.

▲◢

I sat and looked at the telephone. I felt as heavy as lead, as light as air. I felt numb. It couldn't have happened. It couldn't be true. That wasn't Arlene. There had to be some mistake, some confusion, some misunderstanding. I looked around for my cigarettes. It was almost dark in the room. I turned on the bedside table lamp. I found the pack on the floor at my feet. It was crumpled and empty. I got up and went into the bathroom and fixed myself another drink. I went back and sat down at the telephone. It was hard to remember exactly what she had said. Was it possible that I had mis-

123

understood her? Could she have misunderstood me? It hadn't been a very good connection. I took a swallow of my drink, and had another thought. Maybe she hadn't been alone. Maybe there had been somebody there. Maybe she hadn't been able to talk. I sat and thought about it. It had the ring of truth. It was the truth. I put down my drink, and picked up the telephone.

A man's voice said: "Hibiscus Gardens. Can I help you?"

"This is Mr. Fago," I said. "I want to make a call—a long-distance call."

"Yes, sir. And may I have your room number?"

"I'm in room seventeen."

"And what number do you want to call?"

I gave him the number. I waited. I felt tense with excitement, with relief. The telephone rang and rang.

"Hello?"

"Arlene—this is Chick. I'm sorry if I . . ."

The line went dead.

"You're leaving us?" Miss Rockne said. "And going back up North? In December? Ugh! But I must say you're getting a nice early start. I only got here myself about five minutes ago."

"I've got a long way to go," I said.

"Well—let's see," she said. "Hey!" She lifted a card from her file. "You're two days over the week. I'm going to have to charge you the daily rate on that."

"What?"

"I'm going to have to charge you the regular daily rate," she said. "You're over the week. O.K.?"

"O.K.," I said, and got out my billfold. I remembered the cigarette machine near the door. I said: "And I'd like some change for the machine." Cigarettes were all I needed. There was still enough left in last night's bottle for three or four good drinks. I wasn't interested in food, in breakfast, not even in a cup of coffee. All I wanted was to be on my way. I had a long way to go.

"And six makes one hundred," Miss Rockne said. She handed me my receipted bill. She gave me a wider smile. "Bye now," she said. "And have a nice one."

▲ ◢

I tipped up my glass. Nothing happened. My glass was empty. I pushed it across the bar. The bar was a regular bar, with stools and a brass rail and shiny dark wood, but it didn't look quite right. It made me think of a library —a stage-set library. I sat and studied it. The reason was the back-bar. There was no mirror. It had instead a tier of tiny shelves and the shelves were lined with tiny bottles—the little, one-drink bottles of bourbon and Scotch and ready-made martinis they serve on airline flights. That was interesting. I caught the barman's eye, and pointed to my glass.

"Another bottle," I said. It almost made me smile to say it. "I'll have another bottle of Jim Beam."

He came gliding over. He picked up my glass and dropped it behind the bar. He gave me a pleasant look.

"I don't think so," he said. "Not tonight, old buddy. We got strict laws in this state. I think you've had enough."

▲ ◢

I made a good four hundred miles the next day—to an 8-Day Motel just south of Richmond. My lunch was a package of peanut butter crackers and a Coke. My dinner was a hamburger. I was able to eat almost half of it.

126

I didn't have a drink before or after I ate. I didn't need one. After almost eight hours at the wheel, my mind was already numb enough. I was back in my room and in bed and asleep by eight o'clock. But I dreamed— dream after dream after dream. Arlene was in all of them, moving just beyond my reach, and smiling.

▶◀

The gasoline pump gave its terminal clank, and shut off. The usual terminal spurt of gas ran down the side of the fender. The attendant followed my look. He was a stocky young man with rosy cheeks and a mop of curly red hair. He turned gravely back.

"Yeah," he said. "It's your brake lining, all right. I knew it the minute you drove in. I recognized that— you know—like grinding sound."

"What does it mean?" I said.

"Mean?" he said. "It means it's getting ready to go."

"And then what?"

"When it goes?" he said. "Then you'll be in trouble. You won't have no brake left on that left front wheel. You could total that whole assembly. My advice is get it fixed."

"How big a job is it?"

"It's not too big."

"I mean—how long would it take?"

"I don't really know," he said. "You'd have to ask my brother. If he could get to it this afternoon, I guess you might have it by maybe noon tomorrow."

"Tomorrow!"

"Well, look," he said. "You got to take that wheel apart. You got to fit a new lining. A job like that takes time."

I hardly heard him, but I nodded. I looked through the windshield at the traffic pushing up the Maryland Kennedy Highway, but I didn't really see it. Tomorrow! I couldn't wait until tomorrow. I couldn't wait another day, another night. I was too close to the end, to the truth. I couldn't stop now. I had the feeling it was only momentum that kept me going.

I said: "How long do you think it might hold?"

He stared at me.

"You want to drive like *that?*" he said. "You want to drive your car with a *front* wheel brake like that?"

"I've got to be somewhere," I said.

"Wow!" he said. "I don't really know. I mean—like how far are you planning to go?"

"Long Island—eastern Long Island."

He shrugged his shoulders. "That's how far—a couple of hundred miles? I don't know. I guess you might be able to make it."

▶ ◀

There was a traffic light suspended in the distance up ahead. It was briefly red, then beckoning green. There was nobody behind me, nobody approaching, but I didn't dare risk it. The grinding brake drum drummed its steady warning, and I'd already had too many scares tonight, too many yaws and lurches. I took my foot off the accelerator and gave the brake a gingerly touch. The car dragged and swerved, but I had it in safe control. The light was still green. I coasted through, and took a deep breath, and picked up speed again. But not too much. I knew this road. I remembered that this light was only the first of four on this route around Southampton, and the next was the light at the big North Sea Road intersection. It was maddening, though, to have to creep like this.

I watched the North Sea light coming up. I looked at my watch. It was ten minutes after ten. I remembered that there was a McDonald's just around the corner, and I hadn't eaten since noon. But I didn't make the turn. I seemed to have lost the need for food. I crept across the intersection, and on a block to the next traffic light. I crept through that and the next. I crept through Water Mill. Then I was on the straightaway to Bridgehampton. I climbed cautiously up to forty. Headlights flashed behind me. I edged over and let him pass—a panel truck with one taillight and a "Register Matches, Not Firearms" bumper sticker, doing seventy-five or eighty. I followed his vanishing light into Bridgehampton. The only lights in Bridgehampton were the cold and lonely street lights and the light behind the Venetian blinds at Bobby Van's. The smoky warmth behind the curtains beckoned. It wasn't a real temptation. I was too close now for even a drink. I felt a new and fibrillating clutch of tension.

Arlene had never been out of my mind all day, all

evening. But this was suddenly different. I was suddenly almost there. It was suddenly only a matter of minutes. I saw myself going up the steps and across the porch and the back door opening and Arlene standing there—and what did I say? What was there to say? That she had misled me? That she had lied to me? That she had *used* me? I felt the first real exhilarating scorch of rage. I heard again the click of the phone going dead. Did she think that I would accept that? Did she think that I wouldn't dare to come back? Did she think I was really Fago? Did she think that I would settle for the craven safety of Florida? The little house on Rob Roy Circle, the green shade of the pink-brick garden, jumped into my mind. It gave me a pang that brought tears to my eyes. I was more than cheated and duped. She had made me ridiculous. I gripped the wheel, and fanned rage back to a cauterizing blaze. I had nothing to say to Arlene. She had already told me all I needed to know. I hadn't gone to Florida. She had sent me there. She had always done the sending. She had always been inconspicuously in command. I knew enough; I knew too much. But I wanted to confront her. I wanted to stand and look at her. I wanted to hear her confirm, I wanted to see if she dared to confirm, that voice on the telephone.

Fireplace Road was as dark as the Bridgehampton Main Street. Not only the miles of summer houses but even most of the local houses were dark, and the only light at the School Street corner was the blue night light in the back of Barnes' Store. It was a scene, a strangely remote but familiar scene, that I had never expected to see again. I passed the little Presbyterian church on the Green. The road made its remembered bend, and the narrow black bulk of the Talmadge house came into view. The Talmadges too were in bed. My heart began to thump. And so was Arlene. She sometimes sat up late for something special on television. But not tonight. The house loomed up behind its picket of skeleton trees, and the windows—all the windows I could see— were dark. Well, she wouldn't be asleep for long. Unless — My heart climbed into my throat. Unless she wasn't there. Unless she was gone, already moved away. I had given her all the time she needed.

I swung the car into the driveway. I wasn't cold—I was almost sweating—but my teeth were suddenly chattering. I remembered to straddle the permanent pothole. The headlights raked the familiar ruts, the sheltering maple, the garage. I remembered I wasn't going all the way to the garage. I realized I was going too fast. I stepped on the brake. The car went into a skid, a slide, a swerve. It slewed across the driveway and across the patch of lawn. It rode up the slope of the cellar door. There was a crunch and a splinter of wood. The door gave way. The car, the front of the car, the right front wheel, went through the door with a jolt, and hung there halfway down the cellar steps. But I was all right. Not even a bruise. I was only jammed against

131

the steering wheel. I turned and twisted. The horn gave a strangled beep. I pushed myself free.

I got the door open and hauled myself up and out. The car looked worse than it had seemed from inside. Only a wrecker could move it. One headlight was smashed, but the other was brightly tilted and beamed at the house, climbing the drainpipe, showing the undereaves. I looked at the glare on the bedroom window. Arlene had never been a panicky woman. But I could see her huddled up there in our big double bed—tense and listening, knowing and dreading. I almost laughed. I couldn't have planned a better arrival, a more commanding arrival.

I ran through the beam and around the side of the house and up on the back porch. I tried the door. Locked. I felt for the extra key on the nail beneath the kitchen window sill. There was no key there; there was, of course, no reason now for an extra key. I raised my fist to pound on the door—and pulled back. I almost laughed again. This was hardly a homecoming. I could hardly expect her to open the window and throw down the key. I stood and thought for a moment. Then I jumped off the porch and ran down the lawn, down past the garage, down to the woodshed. I found the door and pushed it open and reached along the wall to the corner and grabbed my ax. I turned and ran back to the house.

I stopped and listened. There was only the deep country silence. I raised the ax. I had seen a thousand doors smashed open in the movies. But how exactly was it done? Did I smash the lock? Did I smash out a panel? Did I use the blade—or the head? I decided it wouldn't make much difference. I turned the blade and swung hard at the upper right panel. It shattered like an egg. I pulled the ax back and reached in and down and released the lock and shoved the door crashing open and found and turned on the kitchen light.

Arlene was standing in the dining room doorway. Her face was white and her hair was wild and rumpled and her flowered robe hung open. She was holding my twelve-gauge shotgun.

▶ ◀

I stood and stared. It was an Arlene I hardly recognized. She had a look on her face that I had never seen before. It was a look that matched the voice I had heard on the telephone.

She gave a kind of sigh.

"My God," she said. "My God—you *are* a fool. You're an even bigger fool than I thought you were. Why did you have to do this? Why couldn't you take the hint? Why couldn't you leave well enough alone?"

I didn't say anything. I stood in the glare of white kitchen light and looked at her—at Arlene, at my wife. I had known, I had thought I knew, but I hadn't really believed it.

"Poor Chick," she said. "How *could* you be so stupid? After all these years, you still surprise me. I thought you would call—I *expected* you to call—and I was ready. I thought you would get the message. I don't see how I could have made myself any clearer. I never dreamed that you would be stupid enough to show yourself back here."

"No," I said. I had to clear my throat to go on. "You made yourself clear enough."

"I thought you would realize," she said. "I thought you had the sense to understand that we were safe and free. I knew where you were. That was all that was necessary. I would never have let you starve." Her face tightened. "If only for Charlie's sake."

"Oh," I said.

"It's true," she said. "You know it's true. Charlie was all we ever really had. And then you killed him."

"Arlene," I said. "Arlene—what are you saying!"

"You killed him," she said. "He wanted to be like you. He wanted to be a soldier with all those medals and ribbons. And you let him go. You didn't try to stop him."

"You bitch," I said. "You really are a rotten woman."

"My conscience is clear," she said.

"Yes," I said. "I suppose it is. I'm sure it is." I looked at her. Her eyes were bright and her jaw was set. "All right," I said. "O.K." I shrugged. "I'm not going to hurt you, Arlene. So you can put away that gun."

"Are you crazy?" she said. "You stay right where you are." She raised the gun an inch or two. "Do you think I'm going to let you walk out of here?"

I tried to stand relaxed and unruffled.

I said: "You're going to shoot me, Arlene?"

134

"I'm a widow," she said. "I'm a woman living alone. I have a right to defend myself against an intruder." I tried to look disbelieving. I tried to smile. I said: "That wouldn't be very bright."

"No?" she said. "You get stupider and stupider. No wonder Lambert Tucker let you go." She moved the gun again. "I don't know who you are. I never saw you before in my life—until you smashed your way into my house. And no one ever will again. There won't be that much left to see. But I'm sure there is some identification in that car you wrecked out there. Or in your billfold. Or somewhere. And the police have probably been wondering whatever became of Edwin Fago."

I said: "You're really going to shoot me?"

She raised the gun to her shoulder.

"In that case," I said, "you'd better take it off safety."

Her eyes moved. The gun barrel dipped and wavered. I swung the ax up and back and around—and let it fly.

The gun dropped, thumped, slid under the kitchen table.

Arlene took a backward step. Her knees buckled. She fell down on her knees and rolled over.

I crossed the kitchen in two strides. Her startled face looked up at me. There was no blood. There was only a kind of dent in the side of her head, just in front of her ear. I knelt down beside her. She didn't seem to be breathing. I found her wrist and felt for her pulse. There wasn't any pulse. She was dead. I was alive, miraculously alive—but Arlene was dead. She was *dead* The bottom dropped out of my stomach. The bottom dropped out of everything.

When I was able, I got up off my knees and went over to the kitchen table and sank down on the nearest chair. I crossed my arms on the tabletop and laid my head on my arms. I still had on my raincoat, still had on my gloves. I turned up the raincoat collar for comfort. I nestled my cheek against the warmth of my gloves. I closed my eyes. I told myself I was resting. I told myself that all I needed was a minute or two of rest. I told myself I could feel myself easing. I could feel my heart beginning to steady, to slow. I listened to it beating back to normal. I told myself I was ready. I told myself I was rested enough. I had to be rested. I had to be ready. I had to get up and get started. I still had my life to save. All I had to do was get started. Arlene had showed me the way.

I drew the curtain a little aside, and looked out the window. The Talmadge house through the bare-bone hedge was still dark, still asleep. But the car—I had forgotten the car. I had forgotten the angled, beaconing, beckoning headlight. I went out and around and switched it off. That reminded me of something else. I reached on to the glove compartment, and felt and found the registration card in its envelope—and left it there. That would be witness enough. And its presence there, its forgotten presence there, was also natural

136

enough. I opened the trunk and got my luggage out and took it over to the garage and loaded it into my own car. On the way back to the house, I took a good look at Fago's car. It looked a little strange, but not, I thought, to a glancing eye, too strange. To anyone passing on the road tonight, it wouldn't look much more than hastily, carelessly parked. It might look that way even in daylight. But tonight, the next hour, the next few minutes, was all that really mattered.

I picked up the gun. Something dangled. It was a police identification tag strung on the trigger guard. I turned the gun gingerly over. I looked at the lock. One hammer was down, but the other was cocked—or rather, half-cocked. It was on safety. It gave me a queasy feeling. I took the hammer off safety and broke the gun open. Two yellow shells flew out. That made me feel a little queasy, too. I gathered them up. I stacked the gun in its usual closet corner and returned the shells to their box. There was no need to do anything about the ax. I knew it was free of any useful fingerprints. I left it to be found where it lay. I didn't look at Arlene. I saw her, though. I supposed I would always see her lying there. I told myself that it could have been me. It wasn't the police who had loaded the gun.

I turned out the kitchen light, and felt my way through the dining room and into the living room and over to the desk. I turned on the desk lamp and opened the middle drawer, pulled it all the way out, and let it fall and spill on the floor. Then I pulled and dumped the other drawers. I gave the litter a scattering kick. I stepped back and looked. The room was eerily altered. It was no longer just a room. I had ravaged it into a scene.

I moved on to the bookcase at the foot of the stairs. I got down the big, battered, blue Bartlett's *Familiar Quotations*. Bartlett went back to the brownstone on Tenth Street, back almost to the beginning, and it had always been our money book, our secret bank. It was where we had always tried to keep an emergency fund of cash. And Arlene had thought to keep it up. There was money there: four twenties and a ten. I took the money and put it in my billfold. I put the book carefully, neatly back. Bartlett wasn't part of the scene.

I started up the stairs. I looked at my watch. There was no hurry, no reason to rush. It was only a quarter to twelve. I had plenty of time. There was no kind of cause for alarm. But I felt a push of panic. It was the house, the place, the night. I took the rest of the stairs two at a time. I went down the hall at a lope, and into the bedroom. I switched on the light and moved over to Arlene's chest of drawers. I found her big marketing pocketbook, and opened the inner purse. The car keys were there and a handful of change, and some crumpled bills: a ten, two fives, and three ones. I added the bills to my billfold and pocketed the keys and the change, and threw the purse and the pocketbook across the room. I found Arlene's red leather jewel box. I didn't want to open it, I didn't want to touch it. I didn't want to see her Kappa Alpha Theta pin. I didn't want to see her silver-link identification bracelet. I didn't want to see the earrings I had bought in Teheran. But it had to be done. I took her gold bracelet and her string of cultured pearls. I took the earrings and tossed them under the bed. My hand touched something else—my watch. The police tag was still attached. I tore off the tag and put the watch in my pocket. I dropped the jewel box on the floor. I pulled and dumped the rest of the drawers. I pulled out a couple of drawers in my chest. I turned out the light and bolted down the stairs.

I heaved the garage doors cautiously open, and looked back at the house. The lights were all out and the back door was closed. It looked like any sleeping house. I looked across at the Talmadge house. It was still dark. I edged into the garage, into the car. This was the crucial moment. I started the engine. I sat and let it idle. I couldn't risk the roar of racing the engine warm. The engine pulsed into a reliable drone. I backed out of the garage by feel, by memory, without lights. I braked and got out and gently closed and latched the garage doors. I got back in the car. The Talmadge house was still reassuringly dark. But I didn't turn my headlights on until I was out on the road and halfway down to the Green.

I looked at myself in the men's room mirror. My eyes were red. My face was gray. I needed a shave. My chin sagged. I felt the way I looked. The paper-towel dispenser was empty. I dried my hands on a wad of toilet paper, and went out. The place was comfortably crowded. There were seven men and two women at the counter, and others in the booths. The clock on the wall showed twenty minutes past six. That gave me a good half hour to kill. I didn't want to get to the Babylon station much before seven, much before the big commuter rush. I sat down at the counter and unbuttoned my raincoat.

The counterman came over with a glass of water and a typewritten menu in a plastic cover. I waved the menu away.

"Just coffee," I said. "Black."

I wasn't hungry. I had eaten my way up the Island. This was my fourth stop, my fourth diner. It was the only way I'd been able to think of to safely stretch a drive of an hour or so into six or seven hours. A man driving alone in the middle of the night didn't often pull over to the side of the highway and park.

The counterman brought my coffee. I lighted a cigarette. It tasted vile. I put it out, and sat and looked at my coffee and listened to the man on my right describe to the man on his right last night's installment of *Tales of the Unexpected.*

▲ ◀

I drove the last few blocks in a flurry of gusting snow. The traffic thickened. It seemed to know the way, and I sat and let it lead. We crawled through narrow sleeping streets. We crawled into an underpass and out. The parking lot opened up on the right. Beyond it, bright with lighted windows, was the big stone mass of the Babylon station, and above it on the high embankment two huffing blue locomotives and a string of silvery coaches stood waiting. I turned into the lot and parked in the first slot I found.

I got out and got my luggage. I started to lock the car —and had an idea. It seemed like an idea. I didn't know much about Babylon, but it looked big enough to support a certain amount of crime. I opened the door and stuck the keys back in the ignition. There was at least a chance that the car would be stolen before it was found abandoned here. That would usefully complicate the search for Fago.

One of the locomotives gave a warning hoot. I cut across the lot, trying to hurry, with my bags bumping against my legs. I bought a one-way ticket to New York, to Penn Station, and dragged myself up the long stairs to the open platform. It was snowing and blowing harder now, and I shivered in my raincoat. The coaches were filling fast, but I found an empty seat and stowed my bags and slid over to the window. The locomotive gave another little hoot. I leaned back and closed my eyes. I was asleep before the train pulled out of the station.

141

I started awake. Somebody was shaking my arm. I smelled bay rum. I opened my eyes. I looked up at a friendly face, at a man in an astrakhan hat and a dark-blue overcoat.

"Hey!" he said. "Wake up! It's the end of the line."

"Oh," I said.

I blinked and nodded and got up. All my bones creaked and cracked. I felt every one of my sixty-two years. I got my bags and followed the crowd down the aisle and through the door and along the dismal plat-form. It could have been midnight or noon. I waited my turn at the escalator. I emerged with the crowd in a dead-end corridor on the Long Island level. I moved with the crowd along to the concourse.

My mind suddenly stirred, suddenly tripped. I slowed and stopped. The crowd surged around me and on—left to Eighth Avenue, right to Seventh, up the stairs to Amtrak. A funny taste came into my mouth. I asked myself now what? I asked myself now what did I do? I put down my bags and stood there. I hadn't thought any further than this. Where did I go from here?

And where did I go from there?

From the East Hampton *Star,* Thursday, January 20, 1977:

142

MURDER SUSPECT TAKES OWN LIFE

Edwin Fago, 59, of Cedar Pond Road, Amagansett, was found dead of a gun shot wound in the head last Friday in a motel in Yazoo City, Mississippi. A .32 calibre revolver from which one shot had been fired lay by his side.

Mr. Fago had been sought by police here in connection with the ax murder December 17 of Mrs. Arlene Crawford Hill, 51, at her home on Fireplace Road, Springs.

Mrs. Hill was the widow of Charles L. Hill, retired advertising executive who killed himself last November.

A former employee of the Town Highway Department, Mr. Fago had recently been employed here as a gardener and yard man. Police said identification was made by a driver's license and other papers found in his possession.

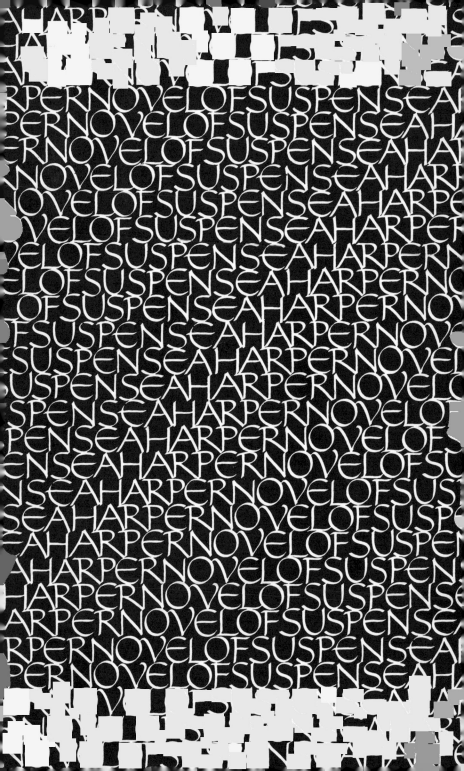